Eva Joly is a Norwegian-born French magistrate and politician. She became famous as an anti-corruption prosecuting judge taking on, among others, former minister Bernard Tapie and the bank Crédit Lyonnais. Her most famous case was that of France's leading oil company – Elf Aquitaine. In the face of death threats, she carried on the case to uncover several cases of fraud. She was chosen by the Green Party to be their candidate in the 2012 French presidential elections. This is her first novel.

Judith Perrignon is a former journalist of the newspaper *Liberation*, a prize-winning essayist and the author of a number of historical and other literary works, including *La nuit du Fouquet's*, co-authored by Ariane Chemin. This is her second novel after the much-lauded *Les Chagrins*, also published this year.

THE EYES
OF LIRA KAZAN

Eva Joly and Judith Perrignon

Translated by Emily Read

BITTER LEMON PRESS
LONDON

BITTER LEMON PRESS

First published in the United Kingdom in 2012 by
Bitter Lemon Press, 37 Arundel Gardens, London W11 2LW

www.bitterlemonpress.com

First published in French as *Les yeux de Lira* by
Éditions des Arènes, Paris, 2011

This book is supported by the Institut Français
as part of the Burgess programme

www.frenchbooknews.com

INSTITUT
FRANÇAIS

A CIP record for this book is available from the British Library

ISBN 978–1–908524–00–3

Typeset by Tetragon
Printed and bound in the United Kingdom by
CPI Group (UK) Ltd, Croydon, CR0 4YY

The Eyes
of Lira Kazan

I

JULY

Abuja, Nigeria

Once upon a time there lived a man called King Okanagba. One day…

"Did they say what time?" his wife asked.

Nwankwo didn't answer. He carried on reading, his daughter on his knee, the book in his hands.

One day the Tortoise went and asked him to sell him two loads of yams. The king replied that he did not want to be paid in money but with nine human heads – the Tortoise should bring him the nine heads by the end of one year! The Tortoise went away, taking the yams, which she ate one by one until there were almost none left. She roasted the last one on the fire and then placed it right at the top of a palm tree…

"Did they say what time?"

"No, the message was to be ready to leave before dawn. That's all. The sun will be up in two hours, they'll be here soon."

"Go on, Daddy!"

A striped rat was passing by and ate it up. So then the Tortoise said: "Since you ate the yam I bought from King Okanagba, you will have to pay King Okanagba with nine heads."

"There's a car coming."

"Stay away from the window, madam," one of the body-guards said.

"I'm still in my own house!"

"Do what they say Ezima," Nwankwo said wearily.

"They're slowing down… How can you just sit there reading stories to your daughter at a time like this?"

11

"Go and wake the other children. Baïna, don't move. We're leaving. I'll go and see what's happening."

Nwankwo got up, unfolding his large frame, and made a sign to the bodyguard: everything must happen calmly. Any more tension would make the whole operation even more difficult than it already was. His wife was nervous, and the children were afraid.

The car had stopped in front of the house, its lights switched off. Nobody got out. The two other bodyguards standing on the porch had their hands in their jackets, ready to draw. The first one went over to the car and tapped at the window. The driver lowered it and mumbled: "*Egbe bere, ugo bere.*" That was the password, an old proverb from childhood days. Nwankwo had often used it: "Let the falcon perch, let the eagle perch." The second guard could alert the family: the evacuation could begin.

The houses all seemed asleep in this residential street in Abuja. Out they came, their luggage carried by servants, first a woman with a child in her arms, then a teenager and finally a little girl holding her father's hand. They looked forwards and backwards and then piled into the big car: they were leaving, not knowing whether they would ever come back, leaving for a long time. The car set off. It had taken hardly ten minutes to abandon everything – their whole life and, soon, their country. Back in the house the sitting-room lights were still on and the book of Igbo fairy tales lay on the sofa.

Nwankwo sat beside the driver and was told the programme. The next stop would be Lagos, where they would discreetly board a speedboat which would take them out to sea to a Norwegian tanker. Three days later they would be on a plane to London.

"But they said we would cross the border and take a plane from Yaoundé," Nwankwo protested.

"Last minute change of plan – this'll be safer," the man replied.

Nwankwo was silent. It would be a long and exhausting journey for the children. His original plan had been to go alone, so as not to condemn his whole family to exile – he wouldn't have been the first African to live so far away from his family. But Ezima had refused.

He turned towards her, murmured that they were going by sea, not the most comfortable of escapes, but the safest. A ship flying a Norwegian flag was less risky than an African road. Then he was silent again, they all were, each one assessing the situation. Abuja was disappearing behind them, with all its glittering modernity. Its cranes, its soulless concrete churches, mosques, office blocks and bypasses bore witness to its youth and new status as capital. It had no history, it was just the artificial shop window for a powerful, oil-rich state. It had replaced noisy, teeming, stinking Lagos. Which was where they were going.

Soon there were no street lights or road markings. Aso Rock melted into the night. *Aso* means victory. The words, the landscape, the doubts – it all churned around in Nwankwo's head. He had believed in victory, he had made powerful men tremble with fear in his office, and he had remained stony-faced against their airs and their threats; he had smiled when they tried to buy him, accepting their fifteen million dollars in hundred-dollar bills, but depositing them in the central bank with instructions to make good use of them, and then pursuing his enquiries with renewed vigour. And then they had started killing his men one by one. Then they killed Uche, his friend and right-hand man. Then they had sacked him and now he was being forced to flee…

"My book!" Baïna suddenly cried. "We've forgotten my book!"

"We'll buy another one," her mother said.

"They won't have it where we're going!"

"They have everything there, you'll see. It's a country with big shops."

"But I want my book! We must turn round."

"That's enough, Baïna!" Nwankwo stopped her. "I've read that story to your brother for years, and so often to you that I know it by heart. And Mummy, too. We'd got to the stripy rat."

He looked at his wife in the mirror. She understood that he needed silence. Ezima shut her eyes and continued.

The rat went off to plant some aubergines. Then the Antelope came along and ate all the leaves. So the stripy rat said: "Since you ate all the leaves on my aubergines and I ate the Tortoise's yam you will have to go and pay the king with nine heads!"

The Antelope galloped away. As she galloped she hit the root of a tree and said: "Root, since you hurt my foot..."

At this stage in the story, when his eldest son was little, Nwankwo had made the sound of the galloping antelope by slapping his hand on his thigh. In those days he had been a young lawyer, a graduate of the University of Zaria. He had handed his diplomas to his father, who had proudly displayed them in his house. "It's good, you've the taste for battle," the old man had sighed, implying that he himself had now lost it. Deep down he had never recovered from seeing those rebels who had fought against colonial power turning into tyrants – it went against all that he wanted to believe about the world and mankind, everything that he thought he had learnt from his beloved books. And then had come the civil war, several military coups and, with the arrival of a whole new breed of predators, he had finally lost his bearings. He was now approaching the end of his life in silence, but it was a silence in which there echoed the sadness of ancient words that had lost their meaning. Nwankwo would visit his father regularly after work, and, sitting on the steps that led up to the bamboo-trellised house, he would tell him about the battles that had become more and more frequent: a newspaper office sacked for having written the truth, small-property owners whose houses had been burnt down to make way for a huge shopping centre. All these cases told the same story: rich country, poor people. Corruption at every level. When a judge condemned a rich man it was only because he would get a larger bribe for the appeal.

Born at the time of independence and the discovery of oil, Nwankwo had been an arrogant and energetic twenty-year-old, but already, behind the rectangular glasses he had worn since childhood, there lurked a serious young man lacking in frivolity, always on the alert – already his life's mission was to do the right thing. The old man always had the last word, with his precise schoolteacher's grammar: "Our country would be better off without this damned oil, I wish that we might never have breathed its odour."

But soon words were no longer enough for Nwankwo. He wanted to act, rather than simply argue in court. He sailed through his prosecutor's exams with brilliant marks. Once again he handed the diploma to his father who this time forgot to frame it and hang it up. Nobody at the time saw any ill omen in this. There at the Nigerian Law School he met Uche, who was his exact opposite, a man who laughed all the time, especially at tragic events. It was an orphan's habit, he would explain. Together they climbed several rungs of the ladder and when, thanks to an unforeseeable political upheaval, Nwankwo became head of the fraud squad, he asked to have Uche at his side. This was five years ago. Now Uche was dead. He had been found with his hands tied, shot through the head, in the boot of his car, two weeks ago. Nwankwo had got the message. The noose was tightening. It was time to leave, and fast.

The road was becoming bumpier as they plunged deeper and deeper into the bush. Nwankwo could sense the silent thickets around them, permanently dripping in this rainy season. Fireflies glittered in the night, like the eyes of a thousand cats watching the fleeing car. Or spirits – the ones that only come out at night. Nwankwo had been told every day, when he was very small: never go outside after sunset, even if someone calls your name; start being cautious in the afternoon, because the land only belongs to men in the morning, and after that they have to share it. The spirits begin to prowl; they take control of the paths, the lanes and the roads. "The toad never goes out in the afternoon – for good reason," his grandfather would say with the affectionate pat that always accompanied his wise sayings. As a little boy, Nwankwo had believed these stories, less so of course as he grew up, but he had never completely freed himself from them. Those who say they don't believe in spirits are lying. On this particular evening he understood those words: the more you try to escape the more they cling to you; leaving forces you to remember and finally to decipher the voices of ancestors and their spells. Man is not king on earth.

In the back Ezima's voice was becoming fainter at the end of the story. The root had hit the antelope's foot, the hawk had touched the root, the child had touched the hawk, then cried and gone to his mother.

"I touched the hawk which touched the root which hit the foot of the Antelope which ate the leaves of the aubergine which belonged to the stripy rat which ate the Tortoise's yam, and now you have to go and pay King Okanagba with nine heads!"

His mother cried: "What! Just because I asked my child a question I have to pay King Okanagba with nine heads, for some yams that were eaten God knows when?"

Usually Ezima would pretend to be angry and the children would laugh. But now, tired, she just whispered automatically with no expression. She was bitter, sad to be leaving her family and her house. She was angry with Nwankwo for putting them all in danger – they had lived with armed guards for three years now. Six bodyguards standing two at a time outside the house, and even following them to school. The frequent arguments between Ezima and Nwankwo usually ended with Nwankwo pointing at the children and saying: "What I'm doing is for them!" As if he could change their future.

It was he who had changed. He had become as hard as stone. He was impatient and forgot important dates: the children's birthdays, the day they met. When, two years previously, the government had annulled the examination that had made him a prosecutor, simultaneously demoting a whole year's graduates, Ezima had begged him to go back to being a lawyer but he wouldn't hear of it. The government had stripped him of his rank in order to remove him from certain cases and put somebody more compliant in his place. But he would not bow down – he returned to school, with Uche at his side, and successfully passed the examination again. Time, he said, was on his side.

On the day the diplomas were handed out in front of families and children, the police came to arrest him on unspecified suspicion of drug trafficking. They brought out handcuffs; those in power seemed prepared to do anything to eliminate him. And then the other pupils came forward, led by Uche, and formed a circle around him, creating a human shield, driving the policemen back. Nwankwo had tears in his eyes. There seemed to be a sign of hope and revolt in this crowd action, a proof that there was some sort of community. But when he saw his eldest son among his protectors looking so young and frail, not yet a man, in his Sunday best, his happiness faded, leaving him empty and afraid. He could not expose this child. He was the leader of a war that was lost.

Where was Uche now? His grandfather had maintained that the world of the spirits did not welcome those who died a violent death. He would be wandering somewhere between the two worlds, in the cold bush, down the red laterite roads, along with the sick and the suicides and those who threaten travellers. Was Uche out there in the night, a lost and wandering friend? Could he see him running away? Did he blame him? Or would he protect them?

Uche's car had been parked outside Nwankwo's house so that it would be he who discovered the bloodstained body, shot in the head, the face frozen in terror, with open eyes. The body had been arranged in a macabre fashion with the trousers pulled down, as had those of the bodyguard which they had found in a hedge a bit farther away. This was a reference to the rumour that he liked men.

Other investigators had died before him. Each time, Nwankwo, their chief, had gone to the funeral and spoken of their courage to the families. Then he had gone away, leaving the children to fulfil their ritual duties. There were no children at Uche's funeral.

"Uche, you will be my Chi, my double, my guardian angel, my shadow," Nwankwo had sworn, sobbing before the body of his friend.

And now this evening, in full flight, listening to the interminable Igbo story and Ezima's low murmur, he added to himself that he would have the skin of the bastard who had ordered his death. Uche would be allowed to rest in the land of the spirits.

The road was now close to the river, it followed the same path, both heading for the sea. On the back seat Baïna was now retelling the story. Her mother was now silent and exhausted, but the little girl doggedly clung on to every word, the load of yams, the nine heads owed to King Okanagba, as though they were the last remnants of a childhood that she instinctively knew was coming to an end that night.

The little girl had reached the part that usually made her shriek with laughter: the king's workers had taken off all their clothes, and the king's wife cried: "Hey! Are you all going to work stark naked now?" But Baïna couldn't laugh this time because she was telling the story to herself. Her mother was at the end of her strength and her father seemed too preoccupied to think of her. She recognized that absorbed expression, that way he had of not being present – there was nothing new about that. In her eight years' experience, she felt that that was how she had always seen him. The day he had announced "We're leaving!" her younger sister Ima hadn't understood, Tadjou had complained that he didn't want to leave his friends, but she, Baïna, had not been surprised. It was as though she had always known it would happen. Her little black eyes had gazed into her father's in agreement. Tonight she felt that he was afraid. He seemed to start every time headlights came towards them.

Nwankwo was tormented by questions. Wasn't this exactly what they wanted, for him to leave like this? To murder him in cold blood as they had done with Uche might have caused trouble, questions from the opposition, stories in the papers. Let him go off and join the exiles! Over there in Europe or the United States he could tell them that half his people lived on less than a dollar a day, nobody would care. Would it have been braver to stay? What would life in exile be like? How long would it last? With a dictatorship, you just had to wait, they always collapse in the end. But with oil a collapse couldn't be counted on for as long as the chain of corruption remained well lubricated. Nwankwo could no longer bear to brood over these unanswerable questions. He listened to Baïna reciting and then joined in. He put on the deep voice of the naked soldiers, as he would have done on an ordinary night, and then carried on to the end of the story.

The king's wife came in. She took off her clothes and hung them round her neck! King Okanagba asked her: "You're bringing me, King Okanagba, my food stark naked, with your clothes around your neck? Aren't you afraid?"

And his wife replied: "You asked me a question; I asked the workers who had replied to the person greeting them who asked

19

a question of the person talking to himself, who asked one of the person walking on his head, who had asked one of the person who was climbing a palm tree on his bottom, who had asked one of his wife, who had asked one of her child, who had touched the hawk who had touched the root which had hit the foot of the Antelope who had eaten the aubergine leaves belonging to the stripy rat who had eaten the Tortoise's yam from the two loads of yams she had got from King Okanagba in exchange for nine heads to be paid in a year – now you'll have to pay yourself the nine heads!"

The king was silent, not knowing what to do.

And together father and daughter recited the last words:

This story tells us that before giving anyone anything you should know if he is a good person and if he tells the truth. The two loads of yams that the king gave the Tortoise are now lost.

Two hours later, Baïna was asleep. The car was silent. They were approaching Lagos. First appeared the lights of the megalopolis, then the damp fetid smell. Mountains of rubbish grew at the gates of the city, at Oshodi, one of the biggest open rubbish dumps in Africa. Nwankwo had visited the stinking scene: rubbish in sedimented strata, with, above it, villages of canvas and plastic in which road menders and their families breathed in the toxic exhalations and fumes. Every day new loads arrived, rubbish and rubble from surrounding areas, but also from the rest of the world, hundreds of thousands of old computers, electronic components and heavy metals unloaded at the port of Lagos and brought to be dumped at Oshodi. And so the rubbish from the north arrived, while the riches of the south were embarked on the oil tankers. Nwankwo pondered all this, haunted by memories. The successful crimes of others represented his own defeats.

It was not yet daylight but the octopus-like city was already awake. Had it ever slept? How many inhabitants were there? Fifteen, twenty million? Nobody was counting any more. As the night ended the daily bustle was just beginning. Already the first traders were setting up their market stalls beneath parasols bleached by the sun, and cars were preparing to join the great traffic jam, the Goslo, which was predominantly yellow, the colour of the town buses. In a few hours' time it would be solid with cars immobilized on the tarmac bridges, throbbing to the sound of Afrobeat music interspersed with the piercing sound of the muezzin, house windows wide open, children everywhere, a compacted crowd covering every square inch of land while street vendors hawked their wares and surreptitiously displayed their contraband merchandise. Nwankwo knew Lagos well as he had lived there before moving to Abuja, a soulless government town. Lagos was terrifying, enormous and dangerous – a monster, but so much more real. Everything was on show, the havoc, the children, the petro-millionaires whose glass buildings overlooked the oily slums. Was it hell or just purgatory? Nwankwo inclined towards hell. In any case it was Africa, with its noise, dancing, dust and crowds.

"For Africans," his father used to say, "being alive means being in a group, and seeing the world through the eyes of the group, all acting together. Life is not an individual enterprise." And yet Nwankwo was leaving.

He turned around and placed his hand on his wife's knee. She opened her eyes at once – she hadn't been asleep. "We're only ten minutes from the port," he said. She nodded and turned towards her eldest son, talking to him gently. The car suddenly stopped and a rough voice called out from the side of the road. A torch shone into the car, onto the children's sleeping faces. A roadblock. The driver said something and the atmosphere immediately relaxed. The policeman's curiosity had been abated, partly by the car's diplomatic status, but mostly by a handful of green banknotes.

Ten minutes later the car stopped. It was time to get out. The children's legs were weak. The luggage was already on the quay. A man stepped forward. Even in the dark one could see deep scars on his face, indicating that he belonged to one of the minority tribes in the north, but enough to scare somebody escaping danger in the early hours of the morning. Little Ima burst into tears when she saw him. The man pointed to a speedboat tied up just below. Nwankwo then said goodbye to his bodyguards, shaking their hands between his, although relations with these men who risked their lives following him remained cool to the end. He saluted the driver too, promising that he would contact the ambassador as soon as he arrived. The family set off towards the edge of the quay.

Nwankwo knew the choppy waters of Lagos harbour well. Pirates sped through them, paid by the local big shots to attack cargo ships, seize the merchandise and resell it to the highest bidder. He had often, when he was in office, sent speedboats out to a tanker that had just raised anchor and was suspected of not carrying the amount declared. Two hundred million dollars a day diverted, Uche had calculated, roaring with laughter. He always said laughter was poison to the lowlifes. It was also his cry for help.

This morning, Nwankwo and his family were the contraband cargo. A tanker was waiting for them out at sea. One by one they disappeared down the ladder, the mother first, then the children and then Nwankwo, as Ima continued to cry.

NORWEGIAN EMBASSY, ABUJA

CONFIDENTIAL

22 JULY

SUBJECT: EXTRACTION OF NWANKWO GANBO

OPERATION TORDENSKJOLD EXECUTED AS PLANNED. NWANK-
WO GANBO AND HIS FAMILY ARE NOW AT SEA ON BOARD THE
TANKER HARALD HAARFAGRE.

GREAT BRITAIN HAS AGREED TO WELCOME MR GANBO AND
HIS FAMILY UNDER THE "JUSTICE NETWORK" PROGRAMME.
HE HAS BEEN OFFERED A POSITION AT OXFORD UNIVERSITY.
HIS CHILDREN'S SCHOOL FEES WILL BE PAID FOR AT A LO-
CAL PRIVATE SCHOOL.

MR GANBO HAS UNDERTAKEN NOT TO PURSUE HIS INVESTI-
GATION INTO GOVERNOR FINLEY AND HIS STAFF WHILE ON
BRITISH SOIL. HE HAS ALSO AGREED TO REFRAIN FROM ANY
PUBLIC COMMENT ON THE GOVERNMENT OF NIGERIA.

OUR CONTACTS IN THE FOREIGN OFFICE HAVE PARTICULARLY
INSISTED ON THESE TWO POINTS. THEY BELIEVE THAT GOOD
ECONOMIC AND DIPLOMATIC RELATIONS BETWEEN THE UNITED
KINGDOM AND NIGERIA ARE OF VITAL INTEREST TO THEIR
COUNTRY.

St Petersburg, Russia

It was always the same in the girls' changing room after training sessions. There were the ones in a hurry who just got dressed and went, the sweaty ones who needed a shower, the chatterers who told you the story of their lives, and Tanya, counting the bruises on her shins and forearms. Lira took off her shoulder straps and guards, wiped away the perspiration between her breasts and then calmly put her clothes on. It didn't take long, just her lace bra, skirt, T-shirt and sandals. It was hot outside. Then she slowly rolled up her black belt and kimono, waiting for the moment when she and Tanya would be the only ones left.

"Hey, battered wife, didn't I tell you to wear shin guards?" Lira said, smiling.

"Clever boots… look at this bruise under my knee, that was you. It really hurt, your *gedan barai*. The rest is Putin. I hate getting him. Look at my leg, I won't be able to wear a skirt for a week now. He always looks as though he's going to kill you just by looking at you."

"He's not called Putin for nothing!"

"He certainly looks like him. He must have come through the KGB – karate's part of the training there."

"Shh! They can hear everything in the men's changing room. If he's really ex-KGB I don't want him to spot us."

"How can you say that, Lira? You've been spotted long ago, you're constantly watched and you're on their files. I don't know why I'm still talking to you…"

"Exactly… Can I come round to yours tonight? I've got to make a call."

"Again?"

"I just want to speak to my daughter for five minutes, not more. I don't want the phone-tappers to start taking an interest in her too."

"What are you thinking?" Tanya said, suddenly more serious as she pulled on her jeans. "Of course they know everything about her already, including the name of her latest boyfriend in Paris! I've read your last article, you know – it's good, but you're looking for trouble."

Lira didn't answer. She leant over the basin and ran some cold water, splashing it on her face. The water smelt of St Petersburg, of stone, metal, of the dark depths of the earth. On rainy days it flowed straight onto the pavements from the giant gutters of the old palaces. Her last piece. It had been so simple to write, no need for research, no long sentences, just a list of the dead from the North Caucasus opposition party: "Maksharip Aushev, Malik Akhmedilov, Zarema Sadulayevna and her husband, Alik Dzhabrailov, Natalia Estemirova." There were shadows lurking behind all these murders, and one in particular, that of Sergei Louchsky, the strong man of the region.

"One day your name will be on that list," Tanya grumbled as she laced up her trainers.

Lira brushed her blonde hair in front of the mirror above the basin. She liked that mirror and always glanced at herself in it after training. She saw in it the reflection of a fearless woman, with a few strands of hair clinging to a still sweaty forehead, the normally pale and hollow cheeks flushed and the eyes still sparkling from the exercise and the fights. She had been doing it for seven years. She was nearly thirty-five. Dmitry, her not yet ex-husband, had mocked her for it.

"Won't your neighbours let you use the telephone?" Tanya was asking.

"No, they say that it's because of me that the whole building is now tapped."

"You swear it's just Polina you're calling?"

"Look, if you think I'd ever put you in the slightest danger, just forget it."

"No, come on!" Tanya sighed, and zipped up her bag.

They left at the same time as the last of the men, including the famous Putin. It was ten o'clock and American music was drifting from the cafés. The men suggested a drink, but the girls declined the offer without even consulting each other, waved and turned on their heels. At the red light, with the crossing light showing eight seconds before it would change, they ran across and disappeared into the underground, carried down the escalators beneath the station's copper-vaulted ceiling.

"Putin's there," Tanya suddenly said.

"I thought he went for a drink with the others."

"So did I."

"Maybe he just felt like going home after all."

"Or maybe he's following us," Tanya replied. "There he is, he's coming right towards us!"

"He's just in a hurry – he wants to overtake us."

"No he's staring at us!"

Putin did indeed stop at their level on the lowest steps of the escalator. He smiled for the first time, and suddenly looked a lot less like the original version – almost sympathetic, even.

"I see we're going the same way. Where are you headed?"

"That way," Lira said evasively, putting out her arm, worried that Tanya would give away her address.

"We get off at Lomonosovskaya," Tanya said, lying with confidence.

They set off towards Line 3 with Putin still walking beside them. He talked about the training session, about how powerful the *yoko geri* move was, a killer kick if you put your strength right behind it. The girls' expressions seemed to say: "So how many people have you eliminated like that?" The corridors were emptier than at rush hour and there was a smell of stale reheated pastry. Tanya seemed nervous. When they reached an intersection she tried to get away.

"Right, well… we're going that way."

"So am I," he said.

And so they found themselves still together on the platform, and then in the same carriage, holding on to the same bar, going nowhere.

"So do you live in the same place?" Putin asked.

"Not far from each other," Lira replied.

There were long silences. At each station the girls thought he would finally get off. Putin hadn't said where he was going, they didn't even know his real name. Lira examined him surreptitiously: he had a flat forehead, receding hair, thin lips that seemed to forbid conversation, and no wedding ring. A woman would normally take that as a sign that he was available, but Lira simply assumed that an agent wouldn't burden himself with a family. It was a bit sad to be eyeing a man, no longer to see if he was attractive, but to find out if he was dangerous. This man was probably just a Russian like her, like all the others left behind by history, proud and ruined and, above all, lost. But Lira was well beyond any regrets for the past.

"Isn't this where you get off?" he suddenly said.

They looked at each other, blushing, and jumped out of the train just before the doors shut.

"Was I distracting you?" Putin shouted.

And he disappeared with the train. They breathed a sigh of relief and burst out laughing.

"Your spy's just your average metro pick-up artist!" Lira giggled.

"Well, be careful. A Mata Hari can be a man. Anyway we're at the wrong end of town now. Back we go."

Lira laughed nervously. She was on edge. It wasn't normal to have to take so many precautions just in order to ring her daughter. It wasn't normal to have to invite herself round so late to the flat of her childhood friend, who was already exhausted by a long day at a museum ticket office.

"I'm sorry about all this," she said.

"Don't worry. A little action doesn't do me any harm after a day of listening to creaking floorboards and old museum attendants' gossip. It was quite fun in the end."

The train screamed through the tunnels and finally the right station appeared with its bright friezes and sculpted garlands along the white vaulted ceiling. Ploshchad Vosstaniya, or the Moscow station because that was where you took the train to the capital. Tanya and Lira ran up the stairs into the fresh air and the pale night, the sky still bright with a few soft clouds at eleven o'clock. On Nevsky Prospect, the last street vendors were still hawking "very good caviar not expensive" to lost tourists. A little farther on, a little old lady sat on the pavement selling apples, flowers and socks that she had knitted. She was also begging. She seemed like a ghost left over from the days of empty supermarket shelves.

Lira and Tanya had lived through those days when they were little girls, and then adolescents. They could remember the feeling of emptiness in this city where the avenues and squares seemed to have been designed by giants; the tarpaulin-covered lorries which would suddenly disgorge uniformed men, the crowded buses where you put your five kopeks into an iron container, watched by the other passengers who acted as conductors. It all seemed so far away. Now the black cars with tinted windows that drove along the Neva and the canals seemed to have appeared in direct succession to the carriages of the past, without the jolts of history, without the town having ever been called Leningrad. Tanya bought a bunch of flowers held by a rubber band from the old woman.

"For my mother," she said.

She lived on Bakunin Prospect. The façade of the building was very fine, redecorated recently, like the whole town centre. But it was another story once you went through the great door – black walls in the courtyard, a jumble of electric wires, cats like tightrope-walkers on the gutters and a permanently ingrained stink of urine. In the corridors flaking paint came halfway up walls on which the stories of love and hate that had passed that way were daubed in graffiti. Tanya stopped at the first floor. Her mother lived there in a *kommunalka*, one of the communal apartments inherited from a revolution that had outlawed all bourgeois comfort and respectability. She handed Lira her keys.

"Just come in and say hello, she'd like that. And then go on up. I'll stay here a bit while you telephone."

Lira followed her. She had already gone in. In Room One Tanya's mother, in a flowery dressing gown, was dozing on a small sofa covered in old teddy bears. In Room Two was the old blind man who had tied strings across the room to guide himself around. Room Three was empty. In the kitchen were three basins side by side – each had their own, with their own dented pans hanging above it, although a homeless piece of soap sometimes wandered from one to the other. Tanya and Lira were greeted with a cry of joy from the old lady, whom they had woken up. They edged between the objects and pieces of furniture, a lifetime's worth, a faded and dusty collection of carpets, fringed lampshades, icons of the Madonna, family photos, a table from the early days of marriage, lace tablecloths. The mother, treating Lira like Tanya, took her face between her hands and kissed her on the forehead. Lira cooperated and then stepped back while Tanya replaced the dead flowers with the new bunch she had just bought.

They could hear objects falling down in the room next-door. The old blind man was coming to join them; nobody ever visited him any more. He appeared at the door near Lira, who was just leaving, took her hand and declaimed in a loud voice:

"A fish said to a man passing by: 'I am the magic fish, I can make your wish come true.'

"'Good,' said the man. 'Supposing I want a million roubles?'

"'I will give them to you, and a palace, too, if you want.'

"'Good!' said the man, drawing up a list of wishes in his head.

"'But you should know that anything I give you I give two of to your neighbour,' the fish warned him.

"So the man put out one of the fishes eyes!"

And the old blind man, still holding Lara's hand, gave a little triumphant laugh, as though it were the jealousy of other men that had deprived him of everything.

Lira finally escaped and went up one floor. She knew her friend's apartment well, with the overloaded cupboard that threatened to crash over in the hall, the bedroom completely filled by the bed, the sitting room whose walls were covered with black-and-white photos taken by her elder brother, who had died in a car crash a few years ago, the cat who shed his fur everywhere, the collection of old American films. She had spent a few nights there at the time of her separation, sleeping on the sofa until she found an apartment. That was three years ago.

She had been the one to leave. She had taken advantage of her daughter's departure for Paris to go too. She had nothing against Dmitry, but for some time she had preferred being in the apartment without him, and she found herself staying later and later at the office. It was a sign that she no longer loved him and needed someone or something else. Behind her were almost twenty years of marriage, during which she had had two brief affairs when on assignments. They had not led to anything and Dmitry had never suspected anything, thinking her too serious, too passionate about her work and absorbed by her subject for that sort of thing. And there had sometimes been other meetings, other friendships that had dissolved without being forgotten

33

for all that. The job, for her, had always meant travel and departure; in the beginning, like so many others, she had imagined herself becoming a great reporter. She loved a scrap and thought she could liven up the dozy editorial offices. It took her some time to realize how inert a newspaper can be, and to learn to manoeuvre her way around sensitive areas and cowardly attitudes. She found herself writing columns instead of crossing frontiers; she covered news items, the politics and the economy of her own vast country, as well as her region and home city. Lira had finally realized that she was living in one of the epicentres of the world. And then, with one assignment north of St Petersburg and less than an hour spent at the site of a huge housing project, her life was turned upside down.

The workers there had downed tools when the management had announced the closure of the canteen and the end of subsidized meals. Such an explosion of anger was a sufficiently rare event in this country to make it worth going up there to have a look. Lira decided not to go through the manager's office to get to the site, she just followed the lorry-tyre tracks that led to the workers themselves. There she talked quietly to them about the empty canteens, all the while observing their torn work clothes and their rusty tools. She had only been there for twenty minutes when one of the management security men, alerted to her presence, grabbed her by the arm and threw her out, shouting "Journalists forbidden!" adding "Bitch" in the way those types did when a woman was not in her proper place. But Lira had seen enough.

It wasn't hard to find out who was backing this two-billion-dollar project. It was Sergei Louchsky, a man close to the top, with billions of dollars of capital, the owner of eighty companies; he controlled petrol, telecom and car companies, as well as several regions in the Russian Federation and a fiefdom in the Northern Caucasus – a nauseating stink of criminality permeated all his businesses. All this was enough to excite Lira – she divided mankind into two parts, the "*sputniks*" and the others. Courageous people on the one hand, and then all the rest.

"Tread carefully," her editor, Igor, had said, knowing as he said it how she would react.

"I know, we must all love the Kremlin, and keep telling them not to worry, we belong to them!"

"Well, I didn't quite say that…"

And then the anonymous phone calls began, the cars drawing up alongside her, the threats passed on by friends who thought they were helping and by others whose job it was to do so. Normally a billionaire wouldn't worry that much when an independent cultural weekly accused him of ill-treating his workers. Why make such a big deal out of Lira? Why did she bother Sergei Louchsky? She didn't let up. When Louchsky opened offices in Manhattan, when he bought an ailing British daily or mines in Africa, when he appeared with his family, with an ex-president of France or with his shirt open at Sochi on the Black Sea, Lira would be watching him, cutting out photos, interviews, financial pieces. She watched him over the years, growing and thriving, surviving all scandal, escaping all the purges. And that was how her life had been turned upside down. Sometimes one single question arose and buzzed through her head taking up all the space: now Louchsky was moving his empire into the City, and so Lira was going to London. "But on one condition, that you tell me who you see, what plane you're on, where you're staying. I want to know where you are all the time," Igor had warned her.

She dialled her daughter's number.

"Polina? It's me."

"Mum! How are you?"

"Good – what about you? Are you relaxing a bit?"

"Yes I've finished revising. I'm catching my breath, it's lovely here, I've been going for walks. I meant to tell you, by the way, I might not come back this summer."

35

"I thought you might not, don't worry. In fact I've got an idea. I've got to go to London in a few days, we could meet, maybe do some shopping, or even go to the sea…"

"Brilliant! What are you doing there?"

"Some interviews…"

"I see. I had an email from Dad the other day, he says you're still messing up your life."

"Well if he's picking on me at least that means he'll leave you alone. Did you tell him you weren't coming for the summer?"

Tanya was back. Lira could hear her busying herself in the kitchen, turning on the radio and the gas. She shouted to Lira, asking how many eggs she wanted.

"Don't worry about me!" Lira shouted back from the sitting room.

Then, to her daughter:

"I'll send you some money and as soon as I get there I'll let you know and all you need to do is get a ticket. The only thing is it'll be a very last-minute decision. Is that OK? It'll be great to be together again. Now I must go, this isn't on my bill."

"OK. Goodnight Mum."

"Goodnight, my darling."

"Supper's ready, Lira!"

They ate together, a few eggs, some bread, cheese and wine. They sat on the floor, leaning against the sofa, because the table was covered with magazines and crumpled laundry. They talked for a long time. It was always difficult to sleep on karate evenings, the body took time to relax; the adrenalin was still coursing around. They talked about everything and nothing, about the old lady slowly dying downstairs, about a pair of too-expensive shoes they'd seen in a shop, about Putin following them, about old love affairs. "Archives, they'll keep their value," Lira said. She had had a bit too much to drink. Tanya told her about her Web encounters.

"And you accuse me of living dangerously! Think of all the nutters out there on the Internet."

"Still, there aren't as many murderers as in your film."

"What film?"

"The one with you as a fearless heroine!"

"I'm just doing my job, that's all."

"Rubbish! You're building up your legend!"

"And you're looking for Prince Charming! The first to get there wins!"

"Neither of us will get there, Lira."

UNITED STATES EMBASSY, MOSCOW

CONFIDENTIAL. REF 01.001537

JULY 15

SUBJECT: FRANCO-RUSSIAN NAVAL COOPERATION

BUSINESSMAN SERGEI LOUCHSKY, A CLOSE FRIEND OF THE
KREMLIN, HAS BEEN OBSERVED FREQUENTLY TRAVELLING
TO FRANCE AND ESTABLISHING HIGH-LEVEL CONTACTS
WITHIN THE FRENCH GOVERNMENT ON THE SUBJECT OF A
JOINT VENTURE BETWEEN HIS RUSSIAN NAVAL CONSTRUC-
TION COMPANY (KUT) AND A FRENCH NAVAL AND MILITARY
CONSTRUCTION COMPANY (DVTS) FOR THE CONSTRUCTION
OF FOURTH-GENERATION LASSEN-CLASS NUCLEAR SSN SUB-
MARINES. ACCORDING TO OUR SOURCES A CONSORTIUM IS
IN THE PROCESS OF BEING PUT TOGETHER BUT THERE ARE
STILL DISAGREEMENTS OVER THE ASSIGNMENT OF MANAGE-
MENT CONTROL. LOUCHSKY WILL NOT SIGN UNTIL THIS
IS SETTLED. WE HAVE SPOKEN TO ALEXANDER DILDTOV,
A HIGHLY RESPECTED DEFENCE ANALYST HERE, AND HE
CONFIRMS THAT IF THE DEAL GOES THROUGH IT WILL BE A
FIRST. WE MUST TAKE ACTION. THERE HAS NEVER BEEN ANY
SIMILAR KIND OF MILITARY COOPERATION BETWEEN RUSSIA
AND A NATO COUNTRY.

Nice, France

Usually by this time Félix had already fetched two coffees from the machine, been through the newspaper with a fine-tooth comb and pored over incoming police reports and dossiers concerning the secret lives of local celebrities. But today he was still buried behind the pages of *Nice-Matin*, in which the lead stories were of an ex-mafioso hit by two bullets and a little girl who had fallen from the tenth floor of a building. The old man had survived, the little girl had not.

"It's always the good who cop it," Félix sighed.

The judge looked up, pleased that his clerk had at last opened his mouth.

"And did you see the bit about Coudry's funeral?"

"Yep. Catholics really deserve their share of the market... All through your life they wipe the slate clean and give you extra chances. And then when it's all over you get a big Mass and you're on your way to heaven!"

It was at times like this that the judge would wonder if he shouldn't just swap desks with Félix. The clerk had a violent temper. At first he had found this tiresome, and had been irritated by this sharp, clever, too-relaxed thirty-year-old, who took the initiative so often and introduced you to his boyfriend without worrying about what anyone might think. Then after a few cases, a few sleepless nights, and days in which they had been subjected to threats – he had once even had a knife held to his throat for a few minutes – he realized that they worked well together and that he felt less alone with Félix at his side. And so he had begun to ignore the difference in rank between them and a sort of tandem had emerged, a partnership between a slightly disenchanted judge and a clerk too clever to be a mere stenographer. Of course scandal-mongers had been quick to take note of Félix's self-confessed homosexuality. Others had asked questions about correct procedure. The Courts were a small place, but the duo had survived by ensuring that everything was always done according to the penal code. The two agreed about everything, but not usually at the same time or with the same enthusiasm. Félix finally folded the paper.

"There's nothing about the banker's wife," he said.

"No, we withheld the information until we could get hold of the husband. He's in the Faroe Islands. And then the results of the autopsy have just come in."

"What do they show?"

"'Death consistent with accidental drowning.'"

"In an evening dress?"

"Yes, hence 'consistent'. Lungs full of water and no sign of violence."

"Alcohol level?"

"1.8 grams."

"Well! When are we going onto the boat?"

"Any minute now, as soon as we get transport. Something wrong?"

"Mark's gone away."

"That was expected, right? Didn't he have a project in London?"

"Yes, but I think we're separating, although nobody actually said so."

"Why do you think that?"

"He took the cat."

Half an hour later the judge, the clerk and the policemen were at the port, stepping onto pontoon number eight. Félix came last, carrying a case containing the computer, the printer, the hole-puncher and the sealing tape. It was already hot outside. He cursed the tourists who wandered around choosing the boat of their dreams; as long as the common man's fantasies were linked to the caprices of billionaires as closely as the minimum wage was to inflation, he and his colleagues would always just seem like heroic toy soldiers. He didn't come from round there, and he didn't like this town. It managed to be both provincial and excessive, its glittering coastline thrust to the fore like a whore's breasts. Nice had always been for sale, money was the dominant attraction; the town had voted against immigrants and had built palaces as winter refuges for foreign kings; it only catered for the rich and powerful.

Félix was forced to stop when the whole procession paused, bumping into each other, to look at the latest arrival in the port, a three-hundred-foot state-of-the-art vessel with a big-bosomed siren on its prow.

"Apparently the owner had his daughter's body moulded to make that…" one of the policemen said.

"That'll give the others ideas! Believe me the next thing we'll see is a big-breast competition!" said the judge.

Félix thought the judge was being surprisingly frisky this morning – he was normally a discreet man who referred to "my spouse" and would have liked framed photos of the children they had never had on his desk and actually blushed when Félix referred to "us gays". The policemen laughed loudly. They were in front of the *Fugloy*, the Stephensens' yacht. The boat was quiet, there was nobody on board. All two hundred feet of it bobbed up and down in the rippling water. There was nothing to be seen on deck. Inside, a teak-lined saloon with cream-coloured upholstery, exactly like that of all the neighbours. There was a sparkling jacuzzi ready for action, polished champagne buckets piled beneath the sideboard. They all climbed on board. Finally a man appeared from behind the glass door, tucking his T-shirt into his trousers and smoothing his hair. He had clearly just woken up. He slid open the door and relaxed when he saw the police. "I'm the captain here," he said in an Australian accent.

45

But he looked horrified when they all stepped through the door, took possession of the eight staterooms and began opening drawers. Félix settled down on the circular white-leather sofa beneath a glass-flowered Murano chandelier; he got out his computer, printer and tapes and placed them all on the low marble table that rested on two crystal balls. The judge explained to the captain that this was an official search. The Australian protested and reached for his telephone. A policeman stopped him:

"No calls from now on. Please empty your pockets. And do not touch anything on the boat."

The captain obeyed. He watched to see that no one over-stepped the mark, while Félix, settled on the white-leather sofa, wrote his formulaic notes: "We presented ourselves at ten o'clock on the thirtieth of July 2010 at the *Fugloy* on pontoon number eight…" He suddenly stopped and roughly pushed aside the cushions behind him with a grimace. The captain grabbed them.

"Watch out, that's coral, mate!" he protested.

Félix gave him a withering look as if to say "Who on earth puts coral on cushions?" Then he got up and followed the judge. There were five bedrooms, each with an elaborate studded and quilted headboard upholstered in fur, linen and leopard skin, with matching paw-shaped lamps. The bathrooms were as you might expect – top of the range, expensive bad taste, with huge tropical-rain shower heads, mirrors with lights set into them and taps made of semi-precious metals. A painting that looked very like a Monet was leaning against the wall in one of the rooms.

"That's worth a few million euros if it's genuine," Félix whispered to the judge.

He saw his own reflection in the huge mirrors on the cup-boards. He hated that insomniac stare. A few more nights like that and he would begin to understand why Mark had left him. Even the judge, who was twenty years older, looked in better shape than him. The mirror was enormous, at least six feet high. Mark used to imitate brilliantly the high-pitched voices of the ladies talking to him about the plans for their villas: "Don't forget my long dresses!"

"Was she alone?" the judge asked.

"Yes," said the captain.

"Show me the logbook, please."

The captain brought a blue cloth-covered book with gold writing. In it was a record of each day's outings, weather and position, and a list of guests, far more numerous than trips at sea. The judge stopped on the last page.

"So there was a small party here on Tuesday evening?"

"Yes, Mrs Stephensen had invited a few friends."

"Were you there?"

"At first, yes. But Mrs Stephensen decided not to go out to sea, so I left quite early."

"What was she wearing?"

"Er… a black sparkly dress, I think…"

"The one they found her in?"

"I don't know."

The judge asked Félix for a photo of the torn dress and showed it to the captain who confirmed it with a slight start backwards. "The usual crowd," commented the judge as he leafed through the log, while Félix pulled some bills and insurance policies out of the drawer of a Louis Quinze commode. "Nothing surprising here. Bath towels: 45,000 euros. Saloon curtains. Eighteen yards silk at 1,800 euros a yard, including VAT. Twenty cases of Louis Roederer Cristal. Let's seize that." The judge agreed. And Félix returned to the coral-embroidered white sofa to complete his inventory. "In the Louis Quinze commode in the second bedroom we found on the left-hand side of the third drawer, the…"

"Who pays you?" the judge asked the captain.

"A company called Swordfish."

"Have you met them?"

"No. Only Mr and Mrs Stephensen."

The judge and his clerk exchanged a look as though to say "You can't fool us". It was the usual millionaire's trick – pretending to be charterers instead of owners.

Back at the office, Félix leafed through the logbook. The names listed were more or less the same as those you found in *Nice-Matin*: the old singer, Sergio, the MP Haudy, in his fourth term, a smooth talker who could go anywhere, a few easy women. Bertaud, king of the heated swimming pool, who was now head of the Chamber of Commerce. Stephanie Douchet, second wife of the ex-president of the region, now the Minister of Defence. There were also people from farther afield: Guy Fielden, a famous gallery owner, and Sergei Louchsky, a Russian nabob with a villa that stood invisible behind the pines on Cap Ferrat. And journalists, former film stars and unknowns – and then wives, first ones, second ones and even current ones.

"They must all have bank accounts, we should go and have a look…"

"Don't start that, Félix, we can't alert the fraud squad every time a rich person drowns," the judge grumbled.

"In a ball dress?"

"They're the only ones who wear them."

An hour later the judge left with a sprightly step. Every Tuesday for the last two years he had been having his piano lesson. He only missed it in extreme emergencies. When he came back he was always in high spirits, happy to be returning to something he had abandoned thirty years earlier. He would put his music on his desk and leave it lying around all afternoon, just to remind people of his connection with Chopin.

Félix remained in his office drawing up summonses for the main witnesses in order of protocol. The judge was right. Félix didn't like these people either, these old bronzed playboys, adult versions of the show-offs who used to exclude him in the school playground. He then sorted through the bills and suddenly realized that he knew the interior decorator who had done the boat. He was a friend of Mark's – they had worked together on several projects. He rang the number on the bill, and the man replied at once. Better still, he told Félix just what he wanted to hear: yes, he remembered that yacht, he had been paid by a company named after a fish, but the banker and his wife had been on his back all the time.

"Terrible taste! I know I should be used to it with all these Russians around the place. But he had fixations, for example he insisted on having cushions embroidered with coral. I said it would be uncomfortable, but he insisted. Usually the men are only interested in the hi-fi and the home cinema, but not him."

"So they weren't just renting it?"

"No way, he was insisting on that fucking coral, it was his boat all right!"

"Can you do me a favour?"

"What?"

"Do you think you could get a copy of the Swordfish cheque from the bank?"

"I can try. How's Mark?"

"I don't know. He's in London now."

GRIND BANK: DISASTROUS FIGURES

The Financial Times, 23rd July

Shares in Grind Bank dropped another 17.5% to £5.25 at the close of trading today. In the last five years the bank's stock has shown one of the most spectacular rises in the financial markets of northern Europe. The bank has just announced the sale to HSBC of its Brazilian subsidiary GBF and it has ceded its 30% share of Norwegian insurance company AWA to AXA, the French group. The company will collect £750m from these transactions. According to the Finance Minister of the Faroe Islands, where Grind Bank is based, the company will now be "in a position to face its refinancing commitments". Investors' anxiety stems from the rushed nature of these announcements and new downward-earnings forecasts for the bank. The bank issued a statement at the end of the morning, saying that "in the context of the global financial crisis, Grind Bank has decided fundamentally to reorganize its activities, focussing now on Russia, Nigeria and Brazil, in order to be in a position to back the growing economies of the twenty-first century." At the end of the day, shares continued to fall.

Tórshavn, Faroe Islands

Sunleif was in front, with the men of Tórshavn. An alert had just been sounded: a shoal of pilot whales was out at sea passing the archipelago; the moment had come to start beating them towards the shore. Already the crowds were hurrying to the beach. Children ran down too – they weren't at school as it was Ólavsøka, the national holiday. Flowers and ribbons had been hung up on the lamp posts. Sunleif had become a man on a day like this. He had been thirteen with blond curly hair and he had killed his first dolphin – there had been blood up to his shoulders – under the proud gaze of his father. Nowadays his hands and muscled arms were as big as his father's.

Sunleif stood up straight. He liked to think that Louchsky might be watching him walking towards the sea. That was why he stood in front, with the locals, gazing at the crowd and at the sea. He wanted his guests, Louchsky and his entourage, and the lawyer Rassmussen, to admire the impressive shape of his thighs beneath the wetsuit rolled down to the waist. He wanted them to see what a colossus he was, carved by the Faroe Islands, at the crossroads of all the winds and currents of the Atlantic.

Last time Louchsky had gone too far, humiliating him in his own house, on his own island. The words still burned through him: "You're my piggy bank! I can smash my piggy bank whenever I want!" the Russian had shouted. And then he had added: "You've got fifteen days, or else…" Or else, what? Fifteen days had gone by.

"On the right, my father's first factories! Eyvin, explain to them!" Sunleif said.

And Eyvin explained to the guests how Stephensen senior had been the first in all the islands to process fish on a large scale. Eyvin was Sunleif's right-hand man, the last of the Viking race, a frail young man who had been through business schools in London and Paris. He calculated and thought fast, knew all the difficult cases by heart, and he knew how to keep quiet and draw up acceptable balance sheets. Today Eyvin's job was to avoid difficult questions.

"Eyvin, have you told them about my father during the war?"

And Eyvin told them about the arrival here of the British, three days after the Germans had invaded Denmark. His father had greeted them and had had the senior officers to stay in his house. He had to save his factory.

Louchsky didn't listen to Eyvin talking. He hated walking and he despised this festive crowd, these women in their long dresses and scarves, and men in caps; their wooden houses were tarred and built close together to protect themselves against the storms and the dark winters. How could he ever have entrusted so much money to that swaggering fool Sunleif in his frogman costume?

They had first met fifteen years earlier in St Petersburg in a gilded nineteenth-century drawing room. It was at the time when Communism was coming to an end and oil was a hundred dollars a barrel. Sergei Louchsky was involved in arranging foreign investments in the gas company. Sunleif, the fish merchant facing him, seemed very recently arrived in his banker's outfit, pulling at his collar as though he was short of air. But if appearances weren't in his favour, the figures were. The fish mogul was opening a branch in London, and then another on the Côte d'Azure; money was pouring in, shares were soaring, rich clients were drawing in more rich clients. Rumours of success grew fast, and the reason was simple: Grind Bank, as it was called, was lending money at rates that undercut any competition, in exchange for which it asked for no guarantees, simply that its borrowers should buy its own shares with some of the money being lent. The bank's shares rose thanks to the bank's own money. Simple, and completely mad. A runaway train. But nobody wanted to see it like that. Caution was not an option, there was no point in it back in the Nineties; growth was vertiginous, banks were offering suicidal loans, and the whole world was caught up in the madness. Louchsky soon saw how useful it could be to put his money there – the little Faroe bank would be a useful laundry, just what he was looking for.

And so for all these years the two men had been giving each other big manly slaps on the back. One would lose the smell of fish, the other the oil stains on his oligarch's outfit. Everything was turned into money. They had got into the habit of meeting in London, in the office of Rassmussen, Louchsky's lawyer, and now Sunleif's. Louchsky never came to the Faroes, until now that things had started to go wrong.

The crowd carried on towards the landing beach, while the men went on to the port, where the motorboats were waiting. They walked through a few more narrow streets, past different-coloured houses, blue, mustard-yellow and blood-red. There was certainly going to be blood. Sunleif hadn't told them exactly what was going to happen that day, he didn't want to spoil the surprise. He was thrilled at the thought of his guests' faces turning as white as their collars when the serious fun began. They had been delighted when he had told them that his rodeo would infuriate the ecologists. These financial sharks were going to see something now, they had no idea. It was a beautiful day, the sea was calm; dark shadows on the water seemed to foretell something, but they were just the reflections of the cliffs, which would one day fall into the sea and disappear. Here the sea destroyed everything.

"Follow me!" shouted Sunleif.

Ten motorboats were ready to cast off. Everybody climbed on board; Louchsky, the lawyer, Eyvin and Sunleif together. The pilot started the engine. Sunleif stripped off his T-shirt, pulled on the top half of the wetsuit and fastened the zip, compressing his fat stomach, as though to indicate to them all "I'm going in the water, boys". Completely unaware of the horrified expression on his guests' faces, he believed in himself as part of a great tradition, that of man against the elements. The boats launched off, with Sunleif's in the lead. He stood, the sun beating down on his already reddening head, shouting over the noise of the engines. He pointed out the islands, naming each one, boasting about their beauty; he told them that to the far north of Tórshavn the land came to an end with enormous precipices from which one can sense on the horizon the edge of the Arctic sea ice. Sunleif was in his element. He had returned to his native land after having made such efforts to blend in at all those board meetings.

"You need months to learn the habits of fish, but only three weeks to become a banker!"

"And just a few days to lose everything," Louchsky muttered between his teeth, but loud enough to be heard.

He was immediately put back in his place by the larger waves outside the bay. He grabbed the handrail, much to Sunleif's satisfaction. He remembered gripping the side of his chair like that when Louchsky had come to threaten him in his office.

"Look over there!" he shouted.

You could just see the shiny dark shadows moving on the water. The dolphins were there. The boats accelerated. A shoal of cetaceans with bumps on their heads could clearly be seen between the waves. It was heading west.

"Gentlemen, the pilot whales! Why pilots? Explain please, Eyvin!"

And Eyvin explained that these dolphins had a habit of accompanying ships, jumping in their wake.

"It's almost too easy!" Sunleif shouted.

The victims were unprepared for their fate. The motorboats took up their positions, encircling the animals, then turned around and began to drive them towards the coast. The dolphins now tried to escape. They turned to right and left, diving down beneath the waves. But the hunters stayed with them, tracking them mercilessly, exhausting them, blocking their way. It took time, not to let a single one escape, but that was the fun of it, the excitement, the roar of the engines over the agility of the beast, the superiority of man over the cleverest of animals. There were yells of excitement on the boats as the men quaffed strong beer. Sunleif had plenty of beer on his boat, but he was the only one drinking. A radio message came saying that two dolphins had escaped to starboard. Sunleif pushed the pilot aside, took the wheel and swung round 180 degrees, shaking the whole boat in pursuit of the fugitives.

"You can't escape Sunleif!"

Another sharp turn and Eyvin just managed to reach over the guard rail to vomit up his lunch. Sunleif sniggered. All around the animals were haggard, terrified and exhausted. They now allowed themselves to be driven towards the shallower waters.

Then you could hear the sound of the metal hooks being raised on the decks. They were heavy, over four pounds each. The pack of hunters had finished their beer and the final assault was about to begin.

"Shit!" Sunleif yelled.

His mobile was vibrating for the fifth time. He answered, furious.

"What? Why am I being disturbed?"

It was the housekeeper, stammering. He said the police had come by, and wanted to speak to him urgently and would wait for him on the beach.

"What do you mean the police?" Sunleif foamed.

He shouldn't have shouted, or looked at the Russian at that moment. Police is police, even in Faroese. Louchsky had had enough of being stuck on this boat with thirty dying dolphins and a gang of retarded Vikings in full carnival costume. He stared at Sunleif and put his hand to his neck in a threatening gesture.

They were both thinking the same: their machinations had finally been exposed, the authorities who controlled the markets and analysed everything were onto them. Sunleif suddenly shivered inside his wetsuit. In his shiny black outfit he looked like one of the big fish floundering in the bay under the hooks, at the end of their strength; he was going to die too, because for him to lose would be to die. The police had come to arrest him, or at least to interrogate him. Nobody on board wanted to go down with him; they all observed him from the other end of the boat. But Sunleif suddenly grabbed his spear and waved it, his neck and shoulders bulging.

"Let the fun begin!" he yelled.

And he plunged the spear into the flesh of the nearest animal, again and again, until the hook caught and pulled it up into the boat. Then he pulled out a foot-long knife and plunged it deep into the dolphin's neck, through the thick layer of fat and flesh. The blade disappeared, then Sunleif plunged his hand in, reaching for the arteries and the nervous system. Blood spurted over the boat, and all the other boats. The sea was now turning red with the dolphins' blood.

The dolphins did not die at once, that depended on the skill of the hunter. Some of the men stayed belching on the boats, others plunged into the water from the beach, carrying hooks; they finished off the stranded animals, pulling them in by their fins, pushing them onto the sand. There was already a pile of thirty or so dolphins, dying or dead, piled up like bags washed up by the sea. The only movements were death spasms. They say in the Faroes that animals die in silence. Others maintained that they could hear cries of pain coming from the cliffs.

* * *

"Go on, Sergei! Take a hook! Straight into the rind!"

Louchsky didn't bother to answer. He had not moved once, and still held on to the handrail. Sunleif had become like an animal now; he threw himself onto a second dolphin that had come up close to the boat, as though begging to be finished off. He jumped into the water up to his waist, bathing in blood; it was all over him – hands, body and face – it looked as though he was himself pouring with blood.

The policemen were waiting there on the beach, two plain-clothes officers, looking a bit stiff, easily distinguishable in the crowd. Each inhabitant would go home with some fat and some meat. Until then the children climbed, laughing, onto the backs of the animals vomiting up their blood. Sunleif, in the water up to his thighs, had seen the men. He was in no hurry, he wanted to bring his great display to an end first. He was the colossus, the chief, the picador and the matador; he was Hercules, the embodiment of all the strength and ferocity of mankind. He wasn't afraid of blood, no, he drank it, he wallowed in it. Let them come! Let the cops come, and the Russians, and all those money sharks, let the blood flow – it wouldn't be his! He still liked to believe that Louchsky was impressed by him.

Finally he stood up and waded out of the water, stepped over the bodies, patted the children kindly on the head: he envied them, having fun riding on a big dead fish, not yet men. He walked, dripping, towards the policemen; his heart was pounding, not from fear of course, it was just his body warming up. Turning round he saw his guests climbing out of the boat, Louchsky in the distance watching him, and he knew what the other was thinking: "You're a dead man if you talk." He knew, too, that it was a lot better to fall into the hands of the police than those of the mafia. He walked through the crowd, greeting his workers. He had to look confident in front of them.

But now the landscape around him suddenly began to seem like a lost paradise. He looked at his father's factories, remembered how he had said "You're a man now" the first time he had waded out of the red water as he was doing today. He saw the white wooden church where he had been baptized and married, and the old Tórshavn primary school, a huge building, now a shop, where he had been the gang leader even then. Beyond, past the corrugated-iron roofs, some of them covered in earth and grass, his own stone house. How many dark winters he had spent here, listening to the breakers sending their salty foam into the steep little streets, dreading the hurricane-like storms. He turned round once more, and for the first time ever, because one only understands death when one gets close to it, he found something macabre in the blue-green Faroe waters turning to red.

The officer stepped forward, clearing his throat. Sunleif turned to face him.

"All our condolences, Mr Stephensen. Mrs Stephensen's body has been found in the port of Nice, in France."

II

AUGUST

The door opened. The judge came in with such a grim expression that Félix thought he might as well spend the fifty-centime piece he had just tossed in the air on a cup of coffee. If it had landed on tails the judge would sign. Now it looked more likely to be heads: the judge would say no. He sat down without a word, tight-lipped, his jaw set. Despite this Félix gathered together the copy of the Swordfish cheque, the address in the Cayman Islands, which hadn't been hard to find, and the plan for an international rogatory commission that he had drawn up while he was at it. He embarked on his report like a child showing off his school work.

"I found Swordfish. Ugland House, South Church Street, George Town, Cayman Islands. You see what I mean…"

"No I don't," said the judge.

"It's the postal address for about 18,000 companies. As Obama said it's 'either the biggest building in the world, or the biggest swindle'."

"Look Félix, I don't care what Obama said, I've got the public prosecutor on my heels. He's taking a personal interest in the case. The people named in the logbook didn't appreciate our visits and have made that known to him."

"Already? News does travel fast. Well, we'll have to work quickly. I've drawn up a request for an international mandate to obtain information about Swordfish. You just have to sign here…"

The judge took the paper and skimmed through it:

29th July 2010. Body of a woman taken from the sea, name Linda Stephensen. 30th July 2010. Search of vessel showed suspicious evidence… important to identify ownership of vessel… to find out who owned the account used for paying decorator… Suspicion of

murder and money-laundering. Request to Cayman authorities
for information vital to inquiry.

"You're a pain in the arse," the judge said, putting down the paper.

"Just sign it! After that you can always promise to go easy on the prosecutor's friends."

"You should shave."

Félix passed a hand over his neglected chin – he could have passed for a conceptual artist at one of the trendy vernissages that Mark used to drag him to. He didn't answer. He knew when it was time to stop. The judge took off his watch, placed it on his desk and began to bury himself in one of the sixty ongoing case files.

Silence fell, broken only by the piercing sound of a drill in the men's lavatories. Then suddenly the door opened and a plump gendarme came in, bearing what Félix enjoyed most about this job: new and unexpected evidence. It was a CD, with Linda Stephensen's name written on the case. Félix grabbed it and slipped it into his computer, with a suddenly humble glance towards the judge, who nodded, and signalled to him to play the recording.

"It's settled, I'm going to divorce him. Why do you smile? You don't believe me… You think I'll never leave my banker husband, the servants, the yacht, the dressing room twice the size of the bedroom…"

"It's just that this is the third time you've announced it."

"I know and each time it's been the same. When I was here I felt very determined, and then as soon as I was back in the Faroes, I became afraid and gave up…"

"Afraid of what? Of him?"

"No, it started even before arriving home. You can't imagine how much the Falcon *shakes, how terrifying the landing at Tórshavn is. There's so much wind up there… I could see the islands through the clouds, there are eighteen of them, I know all their names, at*

66

school we learnt them at the same time as our times tables, as though it would always be useful, as though none of us would ever leave.

"I hung on in the plane, and the more I hung on, the more I gave up the idea of any other plan. I only wanted one thing – to get to the next drinks party in Tórshavn in one piece. And God only knows, you should see what a Tórshavn drinks party is like!

"But this time I'm really getting a divorce. By now Sunleif knows – I left him a message on his mobile last night. I told him I wanted a divorce, that I wasn't going to change my mind, and that we must have a calm discussion. I added that I know plenty about his business. I want my share, I want to be comfortable."

"Did you say why?"

"He can't possibly understand my reasons. Sun is a simple man, he thinks I've had enough of all his mistresses and call girls, in London and everywhere else. If only he knew I couldn't care less about that. Him fucking other women suits me very well – I get left in peace. I'm divorcing him because things have changed. And I've changed too. And it's becoming dangerous..."

"Dangerous?"

"Sunleif has been playing with fire. He's happy, he's got Russian friends, big accounts, oil moguls who put their money with him... It's all going to blow up in his face. Disaster's about to strike, I can feel it, and I don't want to be around when it does.

"Anyway, what matters, Doctor, is that soon you'll be seeing me every week. That's what happens with proper therapy isn't it? I'm going to leave him, and settle here for good. I've got my gallery, people are mad about art these days. I'll negotiate a settlement and then I'm off. It's funny, I've never felt better. And I've never been on the verge of losing everything either..."

The recording lasted about five minutes, and contained nothing but the slightly hoarse voice of a woman speaking French with a Nordic accent, with occasional short questions from somebody who sounded like a psychotherapist.

"Let's summon the husband. And we'll find the shrink to authenticate the recording."

"And while you're at it, why don't you sign for the rogatory commission? At least you'll know why you're getting into trouble," Félix tried again.

"And what are we going to find? Plenty of millionaires' dirty tricks, but nothing about what happened here. Rich people drown too, you know."

"Yes but it's only the poor who can't swim!"

The inquiry moved along fast: the next day it was found that a man had been caught on surveillance cameras at the post office sending a packet. They matched the face against professional lists and came up with a Dr Molny, a psychoanalyst on Rue de Dijon. The police visited his consulting rooms and he gave them further recordings, explaining that he had recorded sessions with Mrs Stephensen's full agreement, as he had with other patients, as part of research he was doing on the early stages of therapy. He asked for complete discretion, as he feared that it would be bad publicity for him.

CD number three. Linda Stephensen was telling the doctor about a dinner party at their house in the Faroes.

"The Russians arrived first, they came early and without their wives. That was a bad sign and Sunleif was surprised. He shut himself up with them in his office. There were raised voices from behind the door. Sergei was doing all the talking. Sergei is a very important man in Russia. He lost his temper. As far as I could make out it was about problems with the stock-market regulators. There were threats too. I wanted to hear more, but the servants were coming and going and I didn't want to be caught like a housemaid listening at keyholes."

Eventually they discovered from the central records four bank accounts in Linda Stephensen's name. The gallery account showed several large transactions, tens of millions of euros sometimes, with Sergei Louchsky's name making frequent appearances.

* * *

Sunleif Stephensen was pouring with sweat when he appeared at the office. He hadn't been far away. He had come to identify his wife's body. He gave Félix a filthy look. Félix studied the other man's appearance: the neck as wide as the head, the shirt buttons stretched to bursting over his fat stomach – not your typical banker. Stephensen stamped over to the judge, wiping his forehead with a handkerchief that he kept pulling in and out of his pocket. He was cursing them in a mixture of English and Faroese – he appeared to be protesting about the search of his boat, about being summoned at a time that didn't suit him, and about being spoken to in this French language that he didn't understand. A frail young man with fading blond curls trotted in behind him. This was his interpreter, whom he called Eyvin.

"Calm yourself, sir," said the judge, inviting Sunleif to sit down.

"What's this circus? My boat is searched, I'm summoned as though I'm a criminal – I'm a busy man!"

"Sir, your wife is dead, so—"

"I know that!"

"…so we're exploring every avenue in order to discover the cause of her death."

"Who authorized you to search my boat? What on earth were you looking for? I thought she drowned!"

"Drowning is certainly one hypothesis. We have begun an inquiry. When it's the wife of an important man like yourself…"

This was the right thing to say to Sunleif. So they hadn't forgotten what an important man he was. Once this had been translated, he began to calm down. The judge quietly opened his drawerful of supplies, which always came in useful during interrogations: alcohol, mints and cigars for the more self-important. For the moment he just handed a tissue to the still sweating Sunleif.

"Please relax, we've got plenty of time. She was a good swimmer, I gather?"

"Yes, very good and she knew the bay well. Her dream was to live here, rather than up there, at home. But she sometimes went out too far and I told her so."

"She can't have gone swimming this time, she was found in her evening dress."

"I can't understand what can have happened."

"When did you last speak to her?"

"Several days ago…"

"What did she say?"

"Just ordinary stuff, bits of news."

"Nothing more?"

"What do you mean, nothing more?"

"Her plans for a divorce, for example."

There was silence. Reactions were slowed down by the intermediary of the interpreter. Especially as the interpreter looked terrified by what he was having to translate.

"No! What's going on here? First they tell me she's dead, now that she wants a divorce!"

The clerk and judge could communicate over the intranet, and Félix sent a note: *The recording?*

"According to our information, she left you a message…"

"A *message*?"

"Listen, Mr Stephensen, you're an important man here, you own a bank, and some of your clients are rich and powerful people. It's quite normal that when your wife is found dead we should ask a few questions."

Note from Félix: *Who does the boat belong to?*

"What have my clients got to do with all this? I warn you that I have informed my lawyer about your intrusion onto my boat."

"That is perfectly normal. What has your relationship with your wife been like recently?"

"Twenty years of marriage, money, demands, journeys, private jets – I don't need to spell it out, it wasn't exactly Romeo and Juliet. But still, we'd built everything up to-gether, we grew up together, we had children together – all that counts, doesn't it? We were very close, we needed each other."

"Did you have a prenuptial agreement? Had your wife asked for a settlement?"

"A settlement for what?" yelled Sunleif.

"Well, a divorce settlement…"

"There you go again with your fucking divorce!"

The interpreter just said "divorce". He looked at Sunleif, terrified. He seemed to be both a loyal servant and a prisoner, a willing but enslaved workhorse. His mouth was still that of a child.

"Listen to this, Mr Stephensen," said the judge.

He signalled to Félix, who started the recording.

"But this time I'm really getting a divorce. By now Sunleif knows – I left him a message on his mobile last night. I told him I wanted a divorce, that I wasn't going to change my mind, and that we must have a calm discussion. I added that I know plenty about his business. I want my share, I want to be comfortable."

Sunleif listened in disbelief, and then suddenly rose and said: "She's not dead?! Linda isn't dead?! I knew it, I was sure. She's somewhere here, and you're digging around in our life and our business? Linda! Linda! It's me, Sun!"

He got up and called her as if she was on the other side of the door. The frail interpreter had stopped translating. The judge and the clerk watched the banker striding up and down the room calling his wife; they hadn't for a moment foreseen this reaction. "Linda, Linda, where are you?" Then he banged his fist on the judge's desk, and leant over him pointing his finger:

"I demand to see my wife. And I demand my lawyer."

A policeman who had come to the rescue gently and firmly forced him to sit down. The judge decided that this might be the moment to bring out the cigars.

"For your wife that's impossible, sir, she's dead, and believe me I'm truly sorry. I thought you had been to the morgue to identify her body."

"Yes but it was her and not her. This is her actual voice."

"Yes, she was seeing a psychoanalyst who recorded it and sent the recordings to us anonymously."

"What do you mean, a shrink? I didn't know... I'm sure she would never have divorced me, you know what women are like, they snivel and moan but in the end they stay. Doesn't yours ever do that?"

The judge quietly closed his drawer. It was a bit soon for cigars. The Viking banker wanted a man-to-man talk. Normally the judge wasn't up for that, but this time he heard himself say:

"Well, yes... Mr Stephensen."

A sly note from Félix: *Do I record this?*

The judge continued.

"She often came to Nice, as you told us. This boat, how long have you had it?"

"The boat... well, we've had it since, well... it's not really ours, we just rent it."

"Who from?"

"Some company, I can't remember the name. We must have the charter agreement somewhere."

Note from Félix: *How did he find out the boat was for hire?*

"How did you know the boat was for hire?"

"An ad in the *Herald Tribune* I think. It was Linda who saw it. She loved being there, and she wanted a big boat, so I said yes, you understand..."

"Look, Mr Stephensen, we can either carry on now or continue this conversation tomorrow. But you will have to tell me more about the boat and the ad in the *Herald Tribune*."

"But I don't know what you're talking about, I don't deal with all that!"

"If you're the owner of the boat, why is it so important to conceal it?"

72

"Stop fucking me around!" (The interpreter preferred "Stop annoying me.")

"When people put property in the name of a third party it's often a way of laundering money."

"What the fuck have all these questions got to do with Linda's death? I've just lost my wife, twenty years of my life, the mother of my children, and now I'm being treated like a petty thief by a little provincial judge—"

"Calm down, Mr Stephensen."

"No, I will not calm down! I will not be trampled on! I know people, you know. You're the one who's going to have to calm down. You're going to regret your slanderous questions."

And, turning to his little frightened robot, Eyvin:

"Translate that properly! Tell him I know people way above his pay grade!"

"Exactly," the judge said, picking up the logbook. "You do seem to have some prestigious connections. What is your relationship with?..."

And the judge then read out one by one the names of those people who had been on the boat the night of Linda's death.

"They're my friends."

"Do you do business with them?"

"For me business and friendship are the same thing."

Note from Félix: *I've got you by the short and curlies.*

"Might one of them have had any reason to harm you or your wife?"

"They're my friends!"

"You wife said in these recordings that your business was going through a difficult patch."

"She didn't understand anything! Just as I don't understand anything about these stupid pictures without paint that she sells for millions of dollars. Each to his own department..."

"What can you tell me about Sergei Louchsky?"

"He's a friend."

"Mr Stephensen, friendships sometimes deteriorate. At least that's what your wife seemed to be saying."

The judge made a signal and Félix turned the voice on for the second time:

"Sergei is a very important man in Russia. He lost his temper. As far as I could make out it was about problems with the stock-market regulators. There were threats too. I wanted to hear more, but the servants were coming and going and I didn't want to seem like a housemaid listening at keyholes. When Sun emerged he was red in the face with great patches of sweat at his armpits. I had never seen or heard of anyone speaking sharply to Sun. Normally it was everybody else who trembled before him, everybody was frightened of him. He went upstairs to change his shirt, I followed him, I told him to calm down, to tell me what was going on. He just pushed me aside. He can throw you to the ground with one hand. That evening I understood that he had lost control of the situation."

Sunleif Stephensen was foaming with rage. If Linda had come to life there and then he would have hit her. Eyvin, beside him, would have given anything simply to disappear.

"Mr Stephensen, we'll stop there for today. However, I am obliged to ask you for your mobile phone so that we can check the messages on it."

"You're joking!"

He got up, unfolding his huge frame, and leant towards the judge, both hands on the edge of the desk.

"Mr Stephensen, you'll get it back as soon as possible. And nothing that is not pertinent to your wife's death will be kept on the file. I'm doing my job, sir."

"Well all right, do it then," the ogre suddenly obeyed, throwing his mobile onto the table.

Two hours later, the commission of inquiry to be sent to the Cayman Islands had been authorized. The serial number of Stephensen's SIM card had been sent to the listening services. The judge, in a filthy mood, pushed open the door to the prosecutor's office – he had been summoned to see him immediately. He was greeted by an over-effusive "my dear fellow" and sat down on an ochre government-issue sofa.

"What's going on with Mr Stephensen?" the prosecutor asked.

"Has he already been complaining?"

"Not just him! I've had the Senator and the President of the Chamber of Commerce on the telephone within the last hour. It appears that you impounded his logbook and his telephone. Isn't that a bit hard on a man who has just lost his wife?"

The judge explained about the recordings and the checks that would be necessary.

"I see. But the autopsy report is quite clear, is it not? Mrs Stephensen drowned."

"Yes, that seems likely."

"So you agree with me?"

"Let's say I don't disagree."

"Good. That's all I wanted to hear. I don't know anything about Mr Stephensen's affairs, but the only thing we're interested in is his wife's death, nothing else. Are we agreed on that?"

"Of course."

"Good. So give him back his telephone and sign the release for the body so that we can have a bit of peace and quiet. You know what these foreigners here are like. They seem to think that because they're helping our economy with their millions we should have to take orders from them. They don't understand that there are procedures that must be followed. Otherwise, all well?"

"Perfectly."

"Your wife?"

"Fine."

"Piano coming along all right?"

The prosecutor drummed his little fat fingers on the edge of the desk. The judge didn't remember ever having mentioned his piano lessons to him.

"It's coming along."

"Good, well I think that's everything… Oh, I was just about to forget the good news! I've done what's necessary to get you the Legion of Honour. In normal circumstances, and I mean normal, it should come through in this Christmas's honours list."

In front of Lira was a transparent building, made entirely of glass, with the thrilling words engraved in white on the sliding doors: Centre for Criminology. She went in. She had just walked through Oxford, hurrying past its domes and towers, unimpressed by the old stones – she had, after all, come from St Petersburg. She now studied the list of departments in the hallway: Security; Sentencing; Crime; Risk; Human Rights; Victims; Prisons; Sociology of Crime; Capital Punishment; Mafia and Organized Crime; Sex, Race and Justice; Strategy of War on Crime; Criminology – a long list that seemed to imply that they were still looking for answers to all these problems.

She asked for Nwankwo Ganbo at the reception desk.

"Third floor, room 352," the receptionist said after looking down the list.

The lift doors opened at once as though eager to be used. The whole building was like a great idling machine lying slumped in the August heat. In the library a few students were writing their reports, but along the corridors the doors opened onto rooms full of empty chairs. One voice could be heard, a not very local-sounding monotone: "Corruption in Nigeria: a multinational company pays costs in bribery case." Lira went towards the voice, and stopped at the entrance to a classroom. The door was ajar and she could see a tall thin black man wearing old-fashioned glasses and a severe expression. He was addressing two students, or rather he was reading the newspaper out loud. This must be Nwankwo Ganbo, of course, this man gritting his teeth as he read the *Financial Times* must be him...

"One of the world leaders in project management has agreed to pay 338 million dollars to settle the lawsuit by the

77

US Department of Justice pertaining to corrupt activities connected with Nigeria. According to financial sources in America, Tevip had been systematically bribing government officials in Nigeria over a period of ten years in order to obtain contracts worth over six billion dollars…"

…a man swept along by world events. He put down the paper and exploded with joy. "A French group in Nigeria pursued by the American justice system, that's good news! They'll prefer to pay up front, so as to cut short the inquiry, that means they'll plead guilty. I've never heard these people admitting to anything." His students listened, open-mouthed. On his desk he had a cube with a photo of a child on each surface, his surely, their bright eyes shining against their black skin. Behind him, like a shadow, he had hung up a huge map of Africa, the land, the rivers, the towns, the deserts, the lakes and little coloured pins by the Gulf of Guinea, his own home.

Lira observed him quietly from the doorway. She liked his tone of voice, very different from that of the average lecturer. This Nwankwo was a real *sputnik*, you could tell. And smart too, with his white shirt and sharply pressed trousers. He must have brought all the files and reports with him, nothing would be forgotten. He must know a great deal about all the arrangements, the money to be made out of Nigerian soil, and about Louchsky himself, who had been a member of every Russian delegation that had come to negotiate access to gas and oil reserves. Nwankwo went up to the map and pointed to coloured pins, like an officer examining front lines in a war.

"These are the areas controlled by governor Finley, the bastard who forced me to go. He was in the pay of Tevip, the company referred to by the *FT*. Just at the moment when sites were being allocated he arranged for regular payments into a Gibraltar bank account. All he needed then was a circuit-breaker to get the money back."

"What's that?" one of the students asked.

"The circuit-breaker breaks the connection between the transmitter and the receiver, the briber and the bribed. Let's take Finley – he charges a large sum for an agreement to mine uranium on his territory, say eight million dollars, the other man creams a bit off as well, that's the game. But there can't be any traces, and so the money is paid into an account in Gibraltar, and that's where the circuit-breaker comes in. He might be a lawyer – he goes to the bank with his power of attorney, draws out the eight million in banknotes in a suitcase, and deposits it in another bank, sometimes just across the road, in an account which this time is in Finley's name."

Alone in the deserted corridor, Lira smiled. Every word Nwankwo spoke seemed to be addressed directly to her, in this curious world in which a Russian and a Nigerian who have never met can find that they have a great deal to talk about. She longed to go in, to listen, to ask questions, but she didn't dare to interrupt the informal but closed circle of teacher and students.

"The other thing the uranium buyer can do," Nwankwo continued, "is to force the seller to raise his price."

"What?" said the students.

"It's a deal: you sell it to me for fifty per cent more than the declared price, you keep ten per cent and the remaining forty per cent is paid into a Swiss commercial account. And so there you are, without anyone realizing it, you have opened an off-shore account."

As he spoke Nwankwo was drawing circles and arrows on the board with a black felt tip.

"You have to try and think like them. Do everything backwards. Start with a criminal act and build a legal structure around it. They are obsessed with one thing only – keeping the money hidden. That's the game, everything must be disguised. It's like a masked ball with us, poor fools, the only ones with our faces exposed. And we have to somehow find our way through it.

Nwankwo no longer spoke in an even, professorial voice. His need to pour it all out was becoming apparent. The black ink on the board was like bile. The two students remained still, willing him to go on.

"There's a Yoruba expression: '*Oyinbo su s'aga!*', which means 'Before he left, the white man shat on the throne'. Our throne is filthy."

"Why did you leave?" one of the students ventured.

Nwankwo put the pen down, and remained for a moment facing the board, as though he wanted to turn his back on the question. Then he turned round and told his story.

"Finley had given the order to kill Uche. Uche was my right-hand man, but above all he was my friend. We had summoned Finley eight days earlier. He came into my office in a foaming rage. He took the chair we offered him but turned it round with his back to us, as if to say 'Talk as much as you like, I'm more powerful than you.' Uche got angry, and coldly asked the governor to turn around, to answer the questions about his bank deposits, but he wouldn't move. Then Uche got up and pulled away the chair and the governor fell down. Uche had knocked down a man used to gazing down at others from high up, from a heavy chair at the end of a long carpet. The governor was on his knees. 'Get up!' Uche shouted, putting the chair straight. 'And sit down!'"

"What did you do?"

"I got up and signalled to Uche to calm down. I didn't want to disown him, but we had to give a bit of dignity back to the governor. We had been much criticized for our methods, and by the opposition as well, and by lashing out like this all we would achieve would be to provide them with a pretext to close us down. I helped Finley up, and I apologized. I know Uche resented that, although he never said so. He didn't have time – eight days later he was dead. They found him in the boot of his car, parked outside my house. I'll never forget his face. He looked terrified and completely alone.

It was his loneliness that struck me as much as his actual death. He had told me to go home early to see Ezima and the children. If I hadn't left him to close up the office on his own, perhaps he would still be alive today. It was all so predictable."

In the corridor, Lira closed her eyes, listening to the pain in Nwankwo's voice. He then returned to his previous didactic tone: "Get hold of the American ruling. It's very important, jurisprudence is in the process of changing," he concluded. The two students left, visibly upset, without noticing Lira flattening herself against the wall.

She tapped three times on the door. Nwankwo was just about to leave. She introduced herself.

"I don't speak to the press, sorry," he said, stepping into the corridor.

"There are just a few things I need to understand—"

"I don't speak to the press. I've got an appointment now."

"I won't quote you."

"Please don't insist."

"I've just got a few questions about Sergei Louchsky. You must have come across that name during your enquiries. He owns a uranium mine in your country."

"The name means nothing to me."

"Could you at least tell me what you know of any contracts with the Russians. Half an hour would be enough."

"Listen, I've only been here for a few weeks. It was a difficult journey, very stressful. My youngest child cried for two hours without stopping in the hold of a boat. The others were quiet but they were afraid too. Now we've got a nice house not far from here, the children are at school, I've got a job. I can't destroy all that."

He was walking fast, and she ran beside him along the empty corridor. His stiff expression betrayed the fact that he hadn't really given up at all. She carried on.

"I repeat, I won't quote you. I've come a long way. I heard a bit of what you were saying just now to your students."

He stopped and stared at her. She shouldn't have admitted to eavesdropping.

"Well then, you've had your half-hour. Goodbye, madam."

She trailed slowly back to the station. The setback was mitigated by a message from Polina with the time of her arrival in London in a couple of days' time. The promise of a bit of light-hearted fun, perhaps a shopping binge at Topshop, cheered her up. Polina was a child of her time, bubbly, sharp and restless. She didn't read her mother's articles – she might do so later, or perhaps not. For the moment she protected herself, avoiding dark areas. She could certainly guess at the seriousness of events around her; when she was little she used to overhear conversations on the other side of the partition – her parents shouting at one another, her father yelling that her mother was sacrificing her family to her work. And she probably agreed with him then. Now all she wanted was to be happy. Lira smiled when she thought about her. She had let her daughter grow up and go away without ever trying to stop her. They had argued as mothers and daughters do, but not about permission to go out – more about random remarks, a question, an over-insistent piece of motherly advice. One day Polina had cracked: "No one is ever up to scratch with you – it's a drag, I've had enough." After that Lira had understood that her desire to get everything right had made her daughter too fearful of getting anything wrong.

The half-empty train gradually filled up at each station. Passengers from the suburbs joined the train as it travelled past the graffiti-laden bridges, the lines of parked wagons, the hoardings: every inch of land was covered. The Thames became thicker and dirtier and soon they were in London, that blend of old and new, curves and cubes, with the big wheel in the distance that seemed to say "This is where we have fun". Lira loved the city. She had loved it long before ever coming here, thanks to the tapes passed around, hidden beneath coats, when she was fifteen. For her it was the home of the Clash, who had given a rhythm to the rage of youth. She had gazed at the graffiti of the time, in those days far more politically driven than now. She had studied albums, photos, the names of the studios; she had learnt the words by heart, pronouncing them perfectly. Listening to rock music and dressing in Western clothes from second-hand stalls had been her own form of resistance as she grew up. Her father would sigh at the sight of her in tight, worn-out black Levi's, not because they represented the great capitalist Satan – he believed that even less than she did – but more because they were so distant from true elegance and high culture, the real thing. That music was just noise, he would say. Lira had spoken to him just before leaving for England and he hadn't even asked her what she was going to do there. All he had done was complain that she had turned down a page in a book he had lent her. She had apologized but that hadn't been enough, he had insisted on giving her a lecture as though she was still twelve years old. His only way of feeling alive was to repeat the same thing louder and louder. Perhaps everyone became like that in the end.

Paddington, the end of the line. Lira decided not to plunge into the Underground. It was already eight and not yet dark. It had been a hot day and this was a good time for a walk. She set off, heading east. She had found a small hotel just beyond Soho; it was not particularly comfortable but the sheets were clean. The brown and beige carpet on the other hand appeared to have absorbed thirty years' worth of dust; the pink walls were hung with bad watercolours of blue lakes and grand houses hidden behind trees – another world, to be sure. But it was central and within the magazine's budget. It would take about three quarters of an hour to get there.

She cursed herself for having gone about things clumsily with Nwankwo Ganbo. On the train, so as not to forget any details, she had jotted down what he had told the students, all the techniques and world-banking mechanisms that were employed to make things presentable. It was all a long way from the official language spoken by the City of London financial analysts and the experts in Russian affairs whom she had spoken to since coming to London. Perhaps she should try to see him again. She was less worried about her article than about having failed to get his attention. She felt that they were alike; she recognized the tension in him. She decided to write down as much as she could that night and go back to Oxford the next day; he'd understand. If she came back, he'd understand. And then Polina would be there. They would go shopping and see the bright lights and the crowds, and eat the Thai food they both loved. They so rarely had a chance to be together.

She hurried on, keen to get to work. There was no table in her room, she would have to work on the bed, sitting on the nasty synthetic flowery bedspread. At Tottenham Court Road, the station nearest to her hotel, she stopped and bought a packet of cakes and a carton of fruit juice to consume while she worked. As she paid, she asked the man at the cash desk the way to the hotel, just to check. Left, and then straight on to the crossroads, the man said, and after that he spoke too fast. Oh well, she'd find it. She turned left onto Charing Cross Road, down Denmark Street towards a crossroads, still thinking about her article. She liked Nwankwo's image of the masked ball. She hesitated, turned right. Perhaps a vampires' ball might be a more effective idea... Suddenly two hands grabbed her shoulders, no, four hands, two men, one on each side of her. She could hardly see them, it was dark now. She pulled away and slapped her attacker's face, scratching with her nails, and kicked her leg in the other direction. But the other man pulled her backwards and threw her to the ground. Thinking she was now at his mercy he leant over her. She kicked both legs into his stomach, pushing him away and getting up, but the one she had scratched was already behind her and caught her by her hair. She shouted but no one heard. She elbowed the first man in the face. He let go. She ran, but not for long. The two men caught her by her jacket and she turned to face them. She caught a hand (protect your face, always protect your face – that's what she had learnt) about to punch her. But then came another blow, and another, and another. She backed against a wall, she didn't know where she was, she shouted as loud as she could. They were surprised by her resistance, but it had only delayed them. They were too strong. She begged them, offered her purse, but they didn't react or say anything. They weren't muggers, or even rapists. They looked at her coldly with tense muscles. One of them searched in his pocket. What was he looking for? A knife? Without thinking Lira launched a kick at his hand, and then the other one became really angry and grabbed her by the throat, holding her against him with his elbow. She could feel his hot beer-laden breath on her cheek as the other one approached, holding the thing he had been looking for. She couldn't see what it was – a little bottle? She saw his grin, a gold tooth and she screamed again. The other man put his hand on her mouth, a window on the street opened and shut again, and then suddenly the burning liquid. Her eyes! She couldn't see, she screamed with pain and collapsed in the darkness. She heard them running away. She heard them speaking – Russian. And then nothing.

It was five in the morning. Félix had slept in his clothes. He stood in front of the sitting-room window. He would have liked to see the sea but the view was obscured by the darkened block of flats opposite. They were all sleeping well, but he had never been able to manage eight hours of unconsciousness. Even when Mark had been there, even when they had been happy. But had they really been happy? After all, he had left. Even then he would often wake up with cramps in his legs, his eyes wide open, full of dark thoughts. He wanted the day to start, to change his shirt and go to the office. There at least things were happening.

"Can we search Louchsky's house?" he had asked the judge the previous day.

"Risky. The prosecutor won't sign."

"You could try getting an emergency warrant from his deputy, order the car for nine o'clock and be off by nine fifteen, you've done it before."

"Well, you might consider shaving, Félix, just in case I do decide to do that…"

He went into the kitchen, made some coffee, turned the radio on, and then off again immediately when all he found was the stock-market report, a series of incomprehensible figures. He sat down in front of his computer, where his email offered him fifty-per-cent reductions on hotels all over the world, loans at criminally high rates of interest, old books, Viagra, but nothing from Mark. He Googled Sergei Louchsky: hundreds of references appeared in French and English. Félix went through them. The man was famous. You could see him already in the winter of 1993, during the great post-Communism car-boot sale of bargain privatizations, shivering at the gates of a factory in Siberia.

He was only twenty-five and he was buying shares from the workers, who had no idea that in two years' time he would be their boss.

The rest was the story of an oligarch surviving purges and battles, always close to those in power, trailing behind him billions of dollars in oil and financial structures all over the world, as well as persistent rumours of corruption and money-laundering. Félix lingered over some of the articles that had been translated from the Russian press. He was particularly interested in a report concerning a bauxite mine acquired by Louchsky. The journalist had repeatedly tried to gain entry to a sinister mining complex. He wanted to find out what had happened to those who had dared to go on strike after the deaths a year earlier of two of their number down the mine. They had refused to come up to the surface, had told of how they were paid according to output, with all production limits and safety rules ignored. "We are serfs," they had said at the time. The article described the silence and the fear that reigned a year later. Voices from behind doors said: "It's better not to talk now." Only one trade unionist would speak, but anonymously. He had holes in his boots despite the cold, and he said that the revolt had cost him dear. He advised the journalist to take care. Félix looked at the byline, that of a woman, Lira Kazan. Her name cropped up frequently. She had written a great deal about Louchsky, his billions, his financial empire, his political contacts and his miserable workers.

Félix arrived at the law courts at five past nine, shaved. The judge informed him that the deputy, barely awake, had signed for the transport. The prosecutor was on holiday. They set off at once, as the order might be countermanded at any moment. They drove towards Saint-Jean-Cap-Ferrat, an area that seemed outside the law, and was certainly unfamiliar to the police services. The most expensive real estate in France, villas were bought and sold through shell companies whose shareholders remained concealed in tax havens. Money could be laundered with total impunity.

This villa was invisible from the road, nestling behind a bank of trees and an iron gate mounted with a moving camera. Through the intercom, a servant informed them that the proprietors were absent. The judge announced himself and said that they had to open up. The gate slowly and reluctantly swung open, controlled from within. There were noises from the pool, and a visibly embarrassed butler advanced towards them, explaining that Mr Louchsky was not there, that his sisters had come with their children. Then a man in a dressing gown appeared, a brother-in-law he said, bald except for two thick, bushy eyebrows. He lost his temper, clenching his fist and grinding his teeth when asked to surrender his telephone. Beside the pool, a row of dazed and dripping blondes in ill-fitting bikinis sat silent and embarrassed.

The judge ordered his team to work fast and to remain totally calm. They were all aware of how unusual it was to be conducting a search in this neighbourhood. Félix searched for a plug, as the police took up their positions and began opening cupboards. Later, at home, round the table with their families, they would laugh about the little lacquer cabinet full of imperial porcelain behind bulletproof glass, the cupboard with 250 pairs of shoes, the dressing room with 120 white shirts and the bathrooms! Madame's had a bathtub in the middle in the shape of a high-heeled shoe covered in pink mosaic, with a giant pair of glass lips on the wall. Monsieur's bath was carved from a single block of marble with, on the wall, a huge man's face in black-and-white pâte de verre.

"That's Louchsky," Félix sighed, stunned by the giant portrait. He recognized him from his Internet searches the night before. And then he thought of the miners in their stricken town. He remembered how Mark had complained about his Russian clients: "It's always the same, they want too much, and all the things they buy just clash with one another! They don't respect anything. They spend a fortune on a whole lot of mother-of-pearl doors at the salerooms and then insist on putting modern dimmer-switches right next to them."

The brother-in-law followed them, the top of his head gleaming more and more brightly. He was no longer protesting but his eyes widened when he saw the judge going into Louchsky's office, sitting down on his chair and trying to open some of the drawers. He went and stood in front of him, stared at him, and ostentatiously put his hand on his neck. The message was clear. It meant you're a dead man, or at any rate a dead judge. The photos in the room conveyed a similar message: Louchsky had had himself framed posing beside all the most powerful men in Russia, here, in Sochi, Moscow or Paris, all in casual or social settings.

Félix knew the judge well enough to notice his expression clouding over. He drew his attention to a painting leaning against the wall.

"Monet. The same one as on the yacht."

"One genuine and one fake?"

"The experts can tell us. One thing is certain, she was doing business with him just before she died."

The judge, Félix and the policemen set off with two automatic pistols, the painting and folders full of documents. They hadn't gone five miles before the judge's mobile rang. It was the prosecutor spitting with rage, demanding an explanation as soon as they got back to the law courts. The judge hung up, not saying anything.

Félix tried to lighten the atmosphere by trying an imitation of the prosecutor. "My deeear friend, you know perfectly well that ninety-eight per cent of cases can be dealt with by the law, two per cent have to remain outside it, and of those two per cent nought point five per cent can be deadly..."

But the judge didn't smile.

Lira woke up. She could smell hospital smells and hear the sound of trolleys and voices on the other side of a partition. It was dark. There was something on her face, a cloth, a bandage. She put her hand up to her eyes, afraid of what she might find. With the tips of her fingers she lifted the bandages, one by one. No light came. The bandage was off, and Lira still could see nothing. Her eyelids wouldn't move. With her right hand she could feel her cheeks, and lumps beneath her eyes. "*Mama, mamoyka*," she murmured, calling for her mother like a child. And then she suddenly remembered the burning sensation and her cries. She cried again. The door opened, a voice approached, close to her, speaking gently in English, telling her she must not touch the bandages, that the doctor was just coming. Then he came. A man's voice, very serious.

"Please stay calm, it's most important. What is your name?"

"Lira…"

"Lira, you came in yesterday. Do you remember? Two young men found you in the street, do you remember?"

"No, where am I?"

"You're in University College Hospital, in A & E. You were attacked. You're going to be all right. But you must keep the bandage on your eyes. I don't know what happened but it looks as though your eyes have been burnt with acid. It's too soon for a definite diagnosis, but your corneas have been badly damaged."

She didn't understand everything he said, but as he spoke, things began to fall into place in her mind. She remembered the danger, the two men, the blows, their voices, their words, Russians.

"Polina, Polina," she suddenly murmured. "Call Polina! She's in danger, she's coming tomorrow."

She tried to sit up, asking for her bag, looking for her phone. The nurse looked around the cubicle and went to ask another nurse who was adamant: Lira hadn't had her bag with her when she had been brought in. She had been found by two young men, she had fainted and they had called an ambulance.

"Polina, Polina," Lira moaned.

The doctor told the nurse to stay with her. He prescribed a tranquillizer and suggested contacting the Russian embassy.

"No!" Lira cried, suddenly understanding. "No, they'll kill me."

The doctor decided to prescribe a stronger tranquillizer. "She's delirious," he said. He went out, instructing the nurse to keep him informed and to put on a new bandage.

"Polina... Polina..."

"Who's Polina?" the nurse asked, leaning over Lira's face, wrapping it again.

"My daughter, she's in danger."

"Is she in England?"

"No."

"Is there anyone here I can call for you?"

"I don't know..." She was crying now. "Yes! At the *Guardian*, the newspaper. Charlotte MacKennedy..."

"Is she a friend?"

"Yes, she's a journalist, like me. Tell her to come quickly."

"OK."

"Call her now, please, I beg you!"

"All right, I will. Just let me finish the bandage."

Once she had done this, the nurse went out. Fifteen minutes later, she came back.

"I got her office, she's not there. I left a message, I said it was urgent."

Lira clutched her hands together on the sheets. She was trembling. Her fingers kept going up to the bandage, and each time the nurse put them back down.

"Keep calm, you're in shock, you mustn't worry," she said as she installed a drip filled with a powerful tranquillizer.

When Lira woke up again a few hours later, Charlotte MacKennedy was there, her hand on hers. They didn't know each other very well.

"Lira, it's me, Charlotte, what happened?"

"Have you told Polina?"

"No, who's Polina?"

"My daughter… she's supposed to be coming… she mustn't come. What day is it?"

Lira's words were muffled and confused. Her mouth was limp. She was sobbing.

"Thursday," Charlotte murmured.

"She's supposed to be arriving tomorrow. You must warn her, tell her not to come, she's in Paris. But don't tell her what's happened, or she'll come anyway. No, she'll suspect. Call her father, that's it. He'll protect her, I'll give you his name, he's in St Petersburg. I can call him if you can get his number. I've lost my bag, my address book, my telephone…"

The nurse came in and said that a woman from the embassy was there.

"I don't want to see her!" Lira cried.

Charlotte rang international directory enquiries on her mobile. She got the number, dialled it, and handed the phone to Lira, who sat up, grimacing with pain: "Hallo, Dmitry, it's me Lira… Listen… Don't shout at me, it won't help, we must work quickly. I've been attacked. But listen! They were Russians, they knew I was here. Be quiet, I beg you! Polina is supposed to come tomorrow, we were going to go shopping together. You must call her and stop her from coming… It's nothing, not bad, but be quiet!" Charlotte watched Lira, not understanding what she was saying to her ex-husband. She remembered calling her when she had been doing a story in St Petersburg. Everybody had told her to get in touch with this famously dogged journalist, a real pest they called her – that was a compliment in the profession. Lira had received her in her agreeably untidy office at the magazine, and they had had lunch together and got along well… "You must get hold of her in Paris, you must protect her. You can blow me up later! Go to Paris now! Stay with her! I'll call you. Yes, I know, it's all my fault…"

She hung up.

"I'm blind, Charlotte, I can't see anything."

"It may just be temporary, you must just wait. This is a very good hospital. Where's your hotel? I'll go and get your stuff."

"12 Bucknall Street."

The hotel entrance was plastered with the logos of travel agents and guides for tourists on modest budgets. The receptionist informed Charlotte that she was not the first person asking to see Lira's room.

"310? The embassy people have already been to collect her stuff. They said she had had an accident, what happened?"

"The embassy?" Charlotte asked.

"They were Russian, anyway," the man said.

She ran up the stairs. The door was ajar, as though someone was still in there, but it was only the chambermaid, who gave an embarrassed smile, indicating that she had nearly finished. The journalist looked around and saw that they had taken everything, the computer, the clothes as well, to make it seem as though they were taking care of her. The chambermaid went, taking the attackers' fingerprints away on her dusters. On the white bathroom tiles was a small plastic bag, with a few forgotten items of make-up. Charlotte gazed at some deep purple eyeshadow, which must have brought out the colour of Lira's eyes in the evening. She didn't take it.

ACID ATTACK ON RUSSIAN JOURNALIST
IN LONDON STREET

The Guardian, 17th August.

Lira Kazan, a journalist for the Russian weekly magazine Mir, *was the victim of a savage acid attack the day before yesterday as she was returning to her hotel in Bucknall Street. She was taken to A & E at University College Hospital. Doctors confirm that her life is not in danger, but are unable to say as yet whether her sight can be saved after severe burns to her eyes. The attackers' methods have led the inquiry to suspect a Russian connection. In the last few years London has become the scene for settlements of scores between various interest groups in Moscow. Scotland Yard, however, did comment as follows: "Normally the Russians don't just threaten, they kill."*

Kazan, 41, has already been subjected to threats in St Petersburg, particularly since she began to take an interest in the growing empire of oligarch Sergei Louchsky. During the last few years the billionaire has been busy distancing himself from earlier underworld connections, and he has recently floated his group on the London Stock Exchange.

The attack on Lira Kazan has only confirmed once again that, for a Russian journalist, it is dangerous, and sometimes deadly, simply to do your job. There is now a long list of similar victims, well known to Lira Kazan, who has recently written an article on the subject. What is new and of particular interest to this newspaper is that they are now being tracked right to the heart of London.

Charlotte MacKennedy

Nwankwo didn't notice it straight away, even though the paper was lying open in front of him. He was listening, fascinated, to his colleague, teacher and researcher Julian Bolton, explaining his paper on 'The sense of insecurity in Europe during the last fifty years'. Bolton seemed to have tamed national anxieties as though they were gales – he could predict when they would rise and when they would die down: public opinion was like a kite in his hands. Listening to him, Nwankwo realized that he was now inhabiting a safe world convinced of its inalienable rights, whereas his own world, Africa, had difficulty in making its feelings and claims heard by anyone. "That sense of insecurity doesn't exist where I come from... But then, neither does a sense of security," he laughed.

And then he saw it. The column on the right-hand page of the *Guardian* seemed to leap at him. "Are you all right?" Julian said. He was trembling. It was her, the girl from the other day; he saw it at once, he remembered what she had said, how she had wanted to speak to him about this Louchsky. "Are you all right?" Julian asked again. Nwankwo looked frightened, slightly mad even. He got up, said "See you tomorrow", and left without any explanation. He ran to his car and set off towards London and the hospital. He was shaken to the core by the idea that he would never be able to save anyone, and even that he was the bringer of bad luck. When he reached the hospital and was asked what relation he was, he just said: "Give her my name, she can decide."

When he came into the room and saw the tiresome girl from the other day now stretched on a hospital bed with her eyes in bandages, he saw once again the bodies of all those friends of his who had been shot down in cold blood. He clenched his fists as a cold shudder swept through his body. He approached; she had agreed to see him and was expecting him.

"Nwankwo?" she asked.

"Yes." He drew up a chair and sat down by the bed. "What happened?"

She told him, her voice weak.

"I was horrible the other day," he said. "If there's anything I can do…"

"No. I don't want to drag you into this. I know what you promised your family. And you're right to be careful – this proves it."

He looked at her, not knowing what to say and yet unable to leave. The nurse knocked again and said the woman from the embassy was still there.

"Tell her to go away!" Lira said.

The door closed.

"I don't want their help," Lira murmured. "They get people killed, or let them be killed and then issue statements saying they will do everything possible to arrest the guilty. I've seen and read that scenario all too often. I must get out of here and escape from them. I don't want to go back. They'd be delighted if I did – I'm dead, or as good as, I won't bother anyone any more…"

Nwankwo listened. What she said about herself applied to him too – "I won't bother anyone any more." He asked if any of her family was coming, and she explained how urgent it was that her daughter should be protected. The nurse came in again, saying that the embassy woman was insisting.

"Tell her to fuck off!" Lira shouted in Russian, loud enough to be heard out in the corridor.

It seemed that not being able to see meant that she was no longer affected by any trappings of power and was now relying purely on her own instincts and certainties. Nwankwo's expression had changed from pity to a hard sparkle. He felt drawn to this woman as to few others. She had sprung, one by one, the bolts on the shackles he had imposed upon himself on arriving in England. He got up quietly, promising to return, saying that she would soon be well, and they would share their secrets. He left the hospital like a man possessed. He tapped "10 Elm Street" into his GPS app, setting everything in motion as he dialled the number on his mobile phone.

"Helen?"

"Yes."

"It's Nwankwo Ganbo. I must speak to you. It's urgent."

"Tomorrow afternoon."

"No not tomorrow, now. I'm on my way."

Fifteen minutes later, Nwankwo entered the headquarters of the Serious Fraud Office.

The first time he had been through these doors had been nearly three years ago, when he was still in charge of the fight against corruption in his country. He had come to Europe to meet the officers who, like him, were tracking the secret millions of dollars poured out by the oil companies. He had repeated his mantra to them all: "If you want to help Africa, you must put an end to this massive corruption. It is at the root of everything – terrorism, civil war, epidemics, they are all merely symptoms of the disease." Helen had taken him to a discreet club with large leather armchairs. They understood one another. They spoke the same language, were accustomed to the slow pace of things, and were infuriated at knowing so much without being able to prove it.

She had told him about her childhood as a diplomat's daughter in Kenya. She had grown up, until the age of ten, in a beautiful house with, beyond, the haunting, spellbinding open spaces of Africa. Then, without anyone consulting her, she had been sent off to a boarding school in Switzerland and had never gone back to Africa. Nwankwo had listened to this woman, still young but with prematurely white hair, thinking to himself that if he had met her as a little white girl in the Nigeria of his youth, they would never have spoken to each other. But here they were, decades later, pursuing the same object. The second time he had met her had been barely a month ago; he had just arrived with his family, wounded but still proud. He had come that time to thank Helen who he knew had helped to get him the job at Oxford.

This time he arrived in Helen's office in a burning fury. He told her about Lira, lying, blind, on her hospital bed. He said that they must help her while she recovered. He asked Helen to protect her as she had protected him. He said they must move fast, that Helen and her staff had the authority to investigate laundering and could trace the recycling of money by Russians and Nigerians in Great Britain. He spoke fast and passionately as though his story and Lira's were already linked together.

"Calm down, Nwankwo. There'll be an investigation, and they may be able to arrest the attackers, don't forget London is peppered with CCTV..."

"What?"

"Surveillance cameras."

"I should think they're already far away. This city is becoming a refuge for people like that. They come and kill people, they dump their money here... Finley's got himself a fifteen-million-pound house, a whole lot of cars including a Bentley, a helicopter – quite a lot for a man on a two-thousand-dollar-a-month salary. You've got to scare them, Helen!"

"Nwankwo, I promise you, we're watching them."

"You must do more than that. Go to the files and get Finley's account details, and Louchsky's. I can help you decipher them."

"I'll see what I can do. But you're a lecturer now, don't forget that, your asylum is conditional on that."

The white wooden church stood at the end of the street, with its red roof and rustproof metal panels. Behind it there was a graveyard without statues, just small crosses and stones on a grass lawn. One of them would soon bear the inscription "Linda Stephensen 1961–2010". Louchsky watched from the back of his limousine, where he could not be seen. He knew that the crowd of mourners held him somehow responsible for her death. That made him smile. He leant back against the headrest.

"You were sleeping with her," he said.

"No!" Rassmussen was startled.

"That wasn't a question, Jonas."

"Well, once or twice."

"More than that, Jonas."

Silence.

"You can fuck whoever you like but not the banker's wife. Now the cops are hovering around, they're going to be asking questions. We didn't need this!"

He opened the door without waiting for a reply. Rassmussen followed him. Together they walked up the path, quietly approaching Sunleif, who was receiving condolences, with his children beside him, who had rushed back from their American universities. Some people simply nodded, others shook his hand warmly. They were a reticent lot round here. Sunleif thanked them in a hoarse voice, watching the Russian and his lawyer approaching. He thought about the five billion dollars they were demanding.

Louchsky came up to him and gave him a firm handshake. Rassmussen's hand was sweaty. They went in without saying anything. They were the last. Sunleif closed the church doors and stood for a moment at the back looking at the rows of mourners. He felt as though he was attending his own funeral. The island people, squeezed on benches at the back, had kept their distance. They knew perfectly well that you were more likely to drown in your bathtub than in a Mediterranean port. The ministers avoided his glance, as though they had completely forgotten the dinners at his house, the loans of private jets, and the envelopes full of cash at election time. As for his children, he didn't recognize them. His son's suit hung loosely on him and his blonde daughter had a diamond stud in her nose. She had insisted on wearing Chinese costume. Their American schools had removed them from their origins; they had lost all interest in fishing and the sea and seemed to be completely indifferent to all the power they stood to inherit. Eyvin was beside them, silent. He was the same age as them and had known them when they were all children, but they had nothing in common now. Sunleif felt a wave of affection for this young employee whom he tormented. He, at any rate, had not forgotten his origins. His affection was increased by the mad and totally illegal act he had ordered Eyvin to commit the night before: "Get into the system and erase everything." Eyvin, as he came into the church, had nodded. He had obeyed.

The banker then took his place in the front row. He was going to say a few words after the pastor had spoken. The service began. Sunleif remembered their wedding in this church. It had been a splendid marriage, between the son of the biggest fishing boss on the island and that year's beauty queen. It had been for better and for worse. And now the worst had happened. He missed Linda, or rather his life with Linda, the beginnings, the rise in their fortune. She spoke English better than him and she had helped him with the early contracts. She even tied his tie. Everything had been so simple then.

And now here she was, stretched out in a flower-decked coffin in the room next door. And while Sunleif was trying to summon up some last words of love, and the pastor spouted impersonal platitudes, as though all lives followed the same course, the dead woman was still talking. Talking too much, far from here, in the office of a French judge and his faithful clerk.

"I live in the middle of nowhere, Doctor, in the Faroe Islands, where they say the gods control the winds. It's a stormy archipelago, with fog, giant waves and long nights. You're always better indoors than out there, and you never ask yourself whether or not you're happy. You just hang on and hope not to get blown away.

"You have no idea how thrilled I was when Sun bought the Falcon*! He bought it just like that, for ten million dollars, for me. 'Linda, you must feel free,' he said. He gave me Magnus and Alf too, handsome pilots in Grind Bank uniforms. He said to them that he was entrusting them with his most precious possession, me. I thanked him, huddling in his arms; men love to feel that they're generous and we're grateful. I knew perfectly well that he couldn't have cared less about my happiness. He just had some money to get rid of. That's what happens when there's too much, well there's never too much, it just sometimes overflows and has to be moved out of sight. I'm speaking too freely. I can to you, can't I? Professional discretion, eh?*

"Anyway, that day all I saw was one figure: four thousand miles allowed on the Falcon*. I just had to ring Magnus and Alf and I could go whenever I wanted. No more timetables, formalities, going through security, other people with their bad breath. With my* Falcon *I could do what I liked. Sometimes I used to go to Paris or London for two or three days, just to do some shopping, or to go to a sale or an exhibition. I go as far away as I can. I can't breathe up there."*

"And here?"

"Here I become somebody else. My skin gets darker, I wear different clothes, I speak another language. I no longer have parents or children – they're all far away. I tell people anything I like about myself. It's like having a parallel life."

"And no husband, or only occasionally."

"It's true, I did love Sun. I loved his strength. I used it. But now it just weighs on me, it's so vulgar. I used to be vulgar too, you know. But I've changed, or at least I'm trying to change. Since I've had the gallery I've met new people and heard new things. Odd what artists talk about."

Two hours later Linda Stephensen was in her grave and the house was full of people. The servants had prepared a huge buffet, wine was poured: they had followed her usual instructions and colour codes. But the guests didn't linger. They drank one glass and looked at the paintings without for once feeling obliged to exclaim about them. The most beautiful thing here anyway was the view of the sea and the hundreds of inlets through the windows.

The Prime Minister had made a formal appearance, and the Finance Minister was still there, in the office. Voices were raised.

"I'm sorry Sunleif, but there's never going to be a good time. So, one more time. What's your plan?"

"Don't worry…"

"Don't treat me like an idiot. The London regulators have been onto us: your bank is failing. The markets have sensed it, the cost of credit default swaps on your paper has soared, the shares are going to collapse at any minute. We should have looked into your books ages ago. We've supported you for much too long."

"It seems to me that I've supported you too."

"If that's your only response, we'll have to remove your banking licence and call in the administrators; there's going to be quite a racket when they lift the lid on your business."

"You'll go down with me."

"In any case we'll all go down if you can't save the bank. The fishermen, the shipbuilders, the pension funds. The whole island will collapse. And the depositors all over the world will be wanting their money back."

"I need five hundred million."

"The government hasn't got that."

"Just five hundred million to avoid the receivers."

"Well, find it yourself, Sunleif! Ask your Russian friends. You've got fifteen days. After that you lose your licence."

The door slammed behind him. Those still in the drawing room pretended not to have heard anything. They soon gathered up their coats and followed the Minister. Quietly they walked away from the fine house that they had so envied in the past, with its splendid gateway whose two columns, with their pediment carved with fish, had once seemed like the entrance to Poseidon's kingdom.

"Say something," Félix muttered.

But the judge didn't reply. He had just read the letter out loud.

Owing to a severe shortage of specialist children's judges and to a worrying increase in juvenile delinquency you have been transferred, in the interests of the effective administration of justice, to the department of minors...

He had put it down, walked around the office, and then sat down with a haggard expression. His head had fallen between his hands. He was like a robot whose circuits were being disconnected one by one. He was fading from sight, they were shutting him down. The transfer would take place the following month. Officially, of course, it wasn't any kind of punishment. But eight days after seeing the prosecutor he was being sent to deal with children – he whose tragedy was never having had any of his own.

"What a gang of bastards," Félix said.

"That's enough," the judge sighed, his head still lowered. He hated coarseness even when things were going badly.

"They're a gang of bastards who'd prefer to have you pursuing thirteen-year-olds selling dope than looking into their mates' crooked dealings!"

Félix was almost shouting. But the judge did not reply.

"We've got a month left – we'd better get a move on!" Félix was getting excited.

"She drowned..."

"No! You don't drown in a ball gown."

"It was embroidered with jewels, it must have weighed a ton in the water, she had been drinking, she slipped and she sank!"

"What about the rest?"

"What about it? All we're investigating is a suspicious death, that's all! The rest is there, but we'd need to search the whole port and raze Saint-Jean-Cap-Ferrat to the ground to find anything. You'd enjoy that, I know, but this isn't a game…"

"I had a reply from the Cayman Islands. They never give out information normally and this time they have. Stephensen's affairs are unbelievable, and Louchsky's even more so!"

"What are you doing in this job, with fantasies like yours? You shouldn't be working in the judicial system."

"I hoped to come across people like you."

"I'm tired, Félix."

"So they've won, then."

"Sorry to disappoint you."

Silence fell. Félix sat raging, twisting the paper clips lying around on his desk into useless pieces of wire. The judge let his telephone ring without answering it. They had reached a critical point in their relationship, almost the end, since their work was the only thing that linked them. This was the moment when they might have lowered their guard and admitted to actual friendship. Two people from neighbouring offices put their heads through the door at intervals of a few minutes. One pretended to be picking up a file, the other asked if everything was all right. Rumours about the punishment had already spread through the law courts. Everybody knew about the procedure: when pressure didn't work, the subject was either somehow compromised or transferred – sometimes both.

Eventually the judge turned on his computer. The usual little jingle of the machine coming on was followed by a few clicks on the keyboard. Félix returned to his study of the Cayman Island dossiers: excerpts from a company's articles of association, a photocopy of Stephensen's passport, extracts from a job lot of bank accounts showing transfers of millions of dollars and euros between Cyprus, Malta, Gibraltar, Austria, Nigeria, Russia…

"It's odd that they're sending us all this," Félix mused, loud enough to be heard. "They don't usually. His wife was right. Stephensen is about to go up in smoke. He's finished."

No reply. Félix remained riveted to the figures. Louchsky's money was there, barely disguised by company names.

"Bingo, Louchsky's all over it!"

Still no reply. Félix went on turning pages.

"Well you're soon going to be busy with something a lot more interesting than kids smoking a few joints."

Silence. This time Félix looked up. The judge had turned bright red, staring panic-stricken at his screen, as though fire had broken out and he didn't know how to put it out. He hammered at the keyboard, turned the machine off, got up, grabbed his telephone and his jacket and rushed out without answering Félix, who had asked if something serious had happened.

After twenty minutes, the judge was still not back. Félix went over to his desk, turned on his computer and accessed his email – he knew the password. Nothing. The judge had deleted the offending message. Félix sat frowning, but then remembered that men over forty-five don't know anything about computer memory. Three clicks later, he found it. The message was entitled "Grand Piano". There were two images: one of a doorway with the number 43 above it; the other was a crude photomontage of a couple having it off against a piano. The man had the judge's greying head and the muscled body of a porn star. Félix smiled briefly at the thought that Chopin had just been an alibi. He had never guessed, and he should have done so. He was pleased to discover a touch of frivolity within the gloomy character he saw each day. But this thought was soon overlaid with fear. The transfer and the intimidation had struck within an hour. Something unstoppable had been unleashed.

* * *

He permanently deleted the offending message and returned to his own desk. It was getting urgent: everything was about to disappear, the judge, the inquiry, the sealed evidence. Félix realized that he would have to photocopy the entire file. He got up and reopened the Cayman files, the ones taken from Louchsky's house, Linda Stephensen's bank statements, the sessions with the shrink. He took out the most important documents, made small piles of them and took them to the photocopier, which turned out to be out of action, like so many things in this building. Shortage of funds, the technical services assured him.

He went up to the next floor and decided to photocopy twenty pages up there every forty minutes, to conceal the fact that he was creating a bombshell. His comings and goings earned him dirty looks from the secretaries, who had never much cared for his casual manner. This time the clerk tried his most winning smile on them. Usually all they got was a witty gibe. By twelve-thirty the pile of documents was ready and the judge was still not back. Félix was worried. He slid the papers into some large envelopes and went downstairs.

He avoided the café which was practically an annexe of the law courts. He wanted to be alone. It was like when he was a child coming out of school: he would run off, without hanging about with the others. He had tried that at first, giggling with the other boys, perched on the backs of park benches, but it hadn't worked. He preferred to go home, to his own games and books, or just to the familiar boredom. He felt the same way now. The courts reminded him of the prestigious Paris *lycée* he had attended, it had the same feeling of decorum, the same splendid staircases. In those days he dressed like a son of the respectable *sixième arrondissement*, worked hard, did everything expected of him. He passed his *bac* with honours, started a law course and allowed his parents to imagine him becoming a judge eventually. Then, one morning, he failed to get out of bed to take an exam. It was the first time that had happened – after that, he gave up the idea of being a judge and trained instead to become a clerk, which was quicker. And at the same time he told his parents that he was gay. His father had declared in a sombre tone, in one of the solemn declarations that were his speciality: "Homosexuality is contrary to social law."

"How true," Félix had said.

He had always thought that if he had been heterosexual he would have taken the exam and passed it. Today he would be a judge, he would be cheating on his wife and letting his superiors pull his strings. What he liked about his judge was that he was what he might have been.

As he walked along he kept trying to call the judge but he couldn't get through. He tried his home, and his wife answered. Félix didn't want to alarm her and just asked, casually, if he had been there. She said no. He walked on through the streets of the old town, making the mistake of turning onto Rue Pairolière: the dense crowds of slow-moving holidaymakers irritated him and he took pleasure in jostling them. He didn't like their shorts and he didn't like the way they seemed to think it was all so authentic. They were just a noisy and common crowd following a beaten track for tourists, awash with olives, clothes shops and nightclubs.

Passing in front of number forty-three he looked up towards the windows as if there might be a chance of spotting the judge in his role of lover, but he reached home none the wiser. As soon as he came in he hid the envelopes in a cupboard beneath a pile of sheets. In the kitchen he found some packets of cheese and ham, and shut the fridge door. It was covered with cards from restaurants stuck on with magnets. He took them all off, they were no longer of any use to him. He wouldn't be going to any of them. Mark was gone, the judge transferred, and there was nothing to keep him here.

He suddenly decided to ring Steffy. Before ten at night he was Stephane Burment, a special advisor at the Foreign

Office, sometimes writing for the Minister himself. Félix had met him on one summer's evening at a villa near Nice. He talked waving his arms wildly as though to make up for the long years of grey suits and imaginary girlfriends. He was a Félix with ambition. That is what had brought them together and then eventually driven them apart. Their affair had lasted for six months with a lot of to-ing and fro-ing between north and south. Nowadays they just periodically exchanged emails usually entitled by Félix: "What's new in the stratosphere?"

"I'll call you back in fifteen minutes," Steffy said.

And Félix imagined him leaving his Empire-furnished office and walking through the corridors, offices and conference rooms, the treasure house and beating heart of the Republic; it was a small world, busy digesting the rest of the world. It operated on two levels, and spoke two languages, the lies loud and eloquent, the truth silent and secret. Steffy functioned like all the others up there, both stiff and supple, always under the threat of a Scud missile and looking for a safer line to follow.

"Does the name Louchsky mean anything to you?"

"Don't tell me you were involved in searching his villa!"

"You've already heard about that?"

"He rang the Minister within the hour. There was a terrible row from the Master of the Rolls's office. Don't say I said so, but your judge is going to be in trouble."

"I know, his transfer came today."

"What about you?"

"I'm just an invisible pawn, a humble clerk... Louchsky and the paintings, does that mean anything to you?"

"Stop this, Félix, it's dangerous."

"Just give me a hint, I'll be all right. No one will know it was you."

"Stop, I'm telling you. Do something else."

"Fuck it, Steffy, we can't just let them get away with it. Can't we just set off a few firecrackers before bailing out?"

"You don't understand! Louchsky's not in the same league as your usual clients. He's into big stuff, oil, gas, arms. He deals directly with the Élysée. He gave the President's wife a big cheque for her foundation only last week. Louchsky is super-well protected."

"I'm not kidding myself, we won't catch him. But I want it to appear in the papers that the judge has been removed from the case. The only track I've got is the paintings."

"Well you can ring Do if you like. He'll probably say the same as me – lie low."

Steffy spoke sharply. They said goodbye and Félix remained sitting on the edge of his sofa. He and that man had been lovers and now he felt he was talking to an official. Do was a gossip. Félix had met him when he was with Steffy, at one of those supposedly avant-garde vernissages where the crowd was only interested in filling their glasses with champagne and spotting celebrities. Do at the time was counsellor to the Minister of Culture. He was an old gay man with dyed hair who gave young men of thirty jobs that should have gone to balding fifty-year-olds. And the Minister had fallen, and Do had gone back to run his legal practice on Boulevard Malesherbes, specializing in art.

Félix waited for a while and then dialled his number. There was no answer. He stammered out an unsatisfactory message, and then looked around him at the apartment that had once been so smartly decorated and clean. He went out, slamming the door behind him, hurrying to see if the judge was back at the law courts.

Somebody else was waiting in his office. Stephensen's interpreter was sitting in the corridor, the blond boy of uncertain age, perhaps older than he looked. He rose, recognizing the clerk, put out a limp hand and said in a weak voice that he wanted to see the judge.

"He shouldn't be long," Félix lied. He could always tell when somebody was about to spill the beans.

He asked him to come in, offered him coffee, did everything he could to put him at his ease. He had no qualifications to hear what the young man had to say, and he rang the judge again, still with no answer, and asked anodyne questions to which Eyvin gave evasive answers. He said he had come to settle some of Mr Stephensen's affairs, the boat, the gallery…

"And he gave you a message for us?" Félix asked kindly.

"Not exactly, it's me… But perhaps the judge should be here."

"We work together… he won't be long. How did you get to know Mr Stephensen?"

"The Faroe Islands are a small place, everyone knows each other. And I went to school with his son before I got the scholarship to come and study in Paris. When I got back I was known as a computer ace, and so one day Mr Stephensen called me at my mother's house and challenged me to test the security of his banking system: 'If you can withdraw a million krónur from my bank, from your house, I'll give you a job.' I did it and he kept his word. Grind Bank was breaking all records at that time."

"At that time? You mean it's all over?"

"Yes… do you know what '*grind*' means?"

"No."

"It means dolphin… When will the judge come? I can't talk without some guarantees. I want protection."

Félix prayed for the judge to come through the door. He couldn't desert so soon, not now!

"Sir, I'm frightened. There's a Mercedes without a number plate that tried to run me down in London two days ago, I'm really scared."

He was crying now. He looked like a child. Félix walked across the office and put his hand on the boy's shoulder. He said gently:

"Listen, it may surprise you but this place is not as safe as you think. Tell me where you're staying. Or give me your number. I'll get the judge and we'll come and hear you straight away."

"Eyvin, 00 44 78 15 54 12."

For years Félix would regret making that promise. An hour later, Eyvin called. He was out of breath, walking fast.

"It's started again, I'm being followed by a car, I don't know where I am."

"Tell me the name of the street."

"I don't know! Er, Rue Blacas – no, Rue de l'Hôtel des Postes." His accent made it hard to understand.

"On the right or the left?"

"I've taken a right turn."

"Go on walking, there are some shops a bit farther along. Go in, I'll send the police."

"They're following me! They're getting nearer!"

"Go in anywhere! Say we're coming!"

But Félix was talking to himself now – the phone had gone dead. He called the police station nearest to where Eyvin had said he was; there was an unenthusiastic reaction so he went upstairs and knocked on the door of another judge's office. The judge was busy, but Félix barged in explaining that an important witness was in danger five minutes away. He begged to get the police to send a team. He would go with them. The judge eventually agreed and Félix ran down into the courtyard, furious with his own judge, who he imagined was at that minute sobbing in the arms of his piano teacher.

All this time Eyvin was creeping through the streets. He eventually went into a shopping mall, ran past a line of cosmetic stands and out by the other door, at random. He felt that every turn he took was crucially important. He hadn't seen the motorbike behind him. He turned left into Rue Paradis, down towards the sea and the big hotels. It was crowded, that was reassuring. He would just melt into the crowds. He called Félix who had just jumped into a police car with flashing blue lights.

"Where are you?"

"I'm going down towards the sea, I think I've lost them."

"But where?"

"I can see the Méridien hotel."

"Go in there. The police will be there in five minutes."

Eyvin jumped at the sound of an accelerating motorbike. It went off in the other direction.

"Everything all right?" Félix asked.

"Yes, false alarm. See you in a minute."

The bike had dropped a man off on the pavement a bit farther on. Eyvin was not alone as he entered the hotel. He went towards the bar, then changed his mind. He couldn't sit down so he walked up and down and then stood next to a vase full of artificial flowers. He felt that everybody was staring at him, that time had stood still. A man was looking at him. He had thin black hair with a cascade of curls at the back of the neck. He looked as though he might be local. Was he a policeman? No, Eyvin realized, telling himself he should run. But he stood frozen. The man came towards him. Eyvin backed away. The man smiled – he had a cigarette in his fingers and looked as though he was going to ask for a light. Eyvin was about to say something when he felt the butt of a gun against his stomach. It was hidden in the man's pocket. He signalled Eyvin to come along with him.

When Félix and the policemen arrived, there was no sign of Eyvin. The staff behind the desk vaguely remembered a young fair-haired man walking up and down. He had gone off with someone, as if they had an appointment, they said. Félix couldn't resist launching a kick at a chrome ashtray that had survived the smoking ban. He heard a bleep in his pocket. A text from Eyvin, that he had prepared in case this happened. The message contained a distant address, and had been sent shortly before he disappeared:

Caliban Towers. Building L. Top floor. Steve.

Sunleif sat on the edge of his bed with his hands on his thighs. He was still wearing the trousers, shirt and socks from the day before. He stared at the cupboard, at the row of suits, unable to decide what armour to put on for the day ahead. Grind Bank shares had plunged by fifty-two per cent the day before. At this rate it would no longer exist when the markets opened. Failure was imminent and no one was even pretending to save face.

His Blackberry vibrated on the bedside table. Sunleif didn't reply. It was yet another message from the Finance Minister, with whom he had spent part of the night. Sunleif had watched him ringing City financiers, the British authorities, Danish, French, American bankers... He had listened to him begging them to help avoid disaster, to save Grind Bank. He had heard him threaten that "a lot of foreign fortunes are going to be wiped out". He had seen him stammering, not quite understanding the replies he was getting. He had heard him promising anything, letting himself be humiliated by the bigger fish: he was a little fish in that pond, a minor politician dealing with a minor bank. And when he finally hung up, Sunleif had listened without flinching as the Minister reminded him of what he already knew, the things he had been praised for in that same office six months earlier: the fact that the public pension scheme and a large part of the Faroe economy was invested in Grind shares. "People are going to lose their homes," he was told over and over again, until one in the morning. It was the first time that real people or proper accounting had ever been mentioned in their conversations. Sunleif had left an hour later without a solution.

He hadn't really slept. He had just lain on his bed reviewing various scenarios. He could put on his funeral suit, still on the back of the chair, and then put a bullet through his head, but that wasn't really his style. Grab the *Falcon* and fly to a palm-fringed beach? They would find him. Anyway, if he was going to live on an island he preferred his own, this one. During the night he had gazed at the silver-framed photo of himself and Linda on their wedding day, remembering the pale cloth lampshade they had had above the bed, before the crystal chandelier. And then he had finally closed his eyes despite the pale light of the midnight sun. His place would be here, at home, when the storm finally broke.

"STEPHENSEN!"

It was Rassmussen shouting from downstairs, drowning out the protestations of Johanna, the housekeeper, who had been unable to prevent him from coming in. He was already on the stairs. Sunleif grabbed the funeral trousers from the chair and buttoned up his shirt. His alarm said 7.16. Rassmussen pushed the door open.

"Get dressed, we're going to the office. We've got some work to do. You fooled us, but it's over… We warned you."

"Jonas, you're in my house!"

"Not for much longer. Look at yourself!"

"Listen. There's a problem with liquidity. If he could put in two hundred million…"

"Shut up and come along."

They went downstairs, Sunleif in front, Rassmussen following, their feet sinking into the thick carpet on the steps. Sunleif could have tossed the lawyer over the banisters with one hand, but today the biggest man was no longer the strongest. They were linked by an unbreakable chain of reciprocal corruption, forced on them by their mutual agreement to do things that could then never be spoken about – the time-honoured Mafia way of doing business. The staff in the house could see how serious the situation was. Their boss now looked like a condemned creature going to its death without a struggle. He had never before left the house without first having his cup of coffee and his boiled egg. Sunleif could feel their stares. Could they even guess at what was going to happen in the next few days? It would all happen very fast. He climbed into the limousine with the darkened windows, and found himself surrounded by armed men. The car roared off. On the side of the road, Eyvin's mother was trudging up towards Sunleif's house, her face ravaged by tears.

The bank was still empty. They shut themselves in the office. Sunleif signed everything. He made over the London headquarters, the offices on the Côte d'Azure, the paintings, the *Falcon*. He worked quickly, as though he was pushing through a deal. Fear and euphoria seemed to be the only two emotions possible when it came to financial dealings.

"We financed your losses, it's natural that we should get the first pickings," Rassmussen said, swivelling around in the rolling chair on the other side of the office. "We couldn't care less how much we get for your assets. The important thing is that you should be stripped bare, reduced to nothing. And don't forget poor Linda's gallery, especially as—"

"Especially as what?" Sunleif said, looking up.

"Nothing. Get on with it!"

Rassmussen was in a hurry. He wanted to be gone by the time all the others started appearing. Government, creditors, investment funds, individuals – they would be besieging the office any minute now. Bankruptcy was imminent. Before he left, the lawyer asked:

"Have you wiped everything clean?"

"It's done."

"No dirty tricks, Sunleif?"

"No. I'll call a board meeting in an hour, and we'll file for bankruptcy."

"If you were planning to do a runner afterwards, forget it. I'm taking the *Falcon* now. I hope the tank's full! You've already lost us enough money…"

He left. His departure didn't mean that they were quits, Sunleif knew that perfectly well. An hour later the offices were full of tense, silent faces. The whole staff was there, prepared for the worst.

"Where's Eyvin?" Sunleif asked his secretary. She shook her head. She didn't know.

The board meeting began. "I'm afraid it's time to say goodbye," Sunleif said. The members of the board of Grind Bank sat around the oval table, silent, their heads bowed. None of them knew much about finance, they had left all that to Sunleif. The door opened and the Minister burst in, breathless, as though he had been running. He didn't even say good morning.

"The Courting Bank wants to make an offer, but first they want to send a team of bankers to go through the accounts. They're on their way."

"You can save them the journey, there are no accounts," Sunleif interrupted him.

"What do you mean, no accounts?"

"Your guys would go into reverse pretty fast if they saw them anyway, so you might as well call them and tell them to turn round!"

"So what do you suggest?"

"You bail us out or we declare bankruptcy."

"The state couldn't cover half of this haemorrhage you've caused, you maniac!"

"So, we file. Gentlemen…"

The men around the table prepared to raise their hands, like doctors calling the time of death. But the Minister's telephone rang again, once more delaying the scuttling of the ship. The Minister, still imagining that a miracle could happen, repeated out loud the demands of the buyer.

"The offer includes a demand that Sunleif Stephensen should be replaced."

* * *

Sunleif gave a great roar of laughter, like an ogre, or a clap of thunder. He was cracking up. He shouted. He waved his arms. He told them to come and look at the accounts if they felt like it. "Let them come! Let them come! Just as long as they like birds, rocks, waves and landscape – that's all that's real here in the Faroes!"

It was a strange sight – a bank adrift, already sunk on the stock-market screens. A minister who pretended to believe that he was in control of his country's economy. A fisherman who thought he was a banker. And bonus-eaters who thought they had diplomas from Harvard Business School. None of them could remember the time when living in the middle of the ocean protected you from epidemics.

Then a woman came in. No secretary or security guard had tried to stop her, they had gone the same way as the bosses. She was Eyvin's mother. She had so often imagined this room with her son in the middle, in a fine suit, with a fine career ahead of him. The morning she had walked all the way there, crying. She collapsed in front of Sunleif, sobbing:

"My Eyvin is dead! Why?"

Postmortem Report:
EYVIN STISSON

The postmortem took place at 11.00 on 28th August 2010. It was carried out by Dr Robert Travis, associate forensic pathologist, in the presence of Detective Chief Inspector Donald Shiff.

The body was discovered by walkers beneath a hedge alongside the A282, 18 miles from London, on the evening of 27th August. The absence of rigor mortis appears to indicate that death had occurred several days earlier.

The body is that of a white male of average build, of around twenty-five years of age, 5 foot 10 inches tall, weighing 150lbs. The dead man was wearing black trousers; he did not have a shirt, socks or shoes. Blond hair, covered in dried blood. Eye colour indeterminable, burnt with acid. Around the eyes are phlyctenae, blisters caused by burning. On the face, several traumatic lesions and contusions, deep purple in colour, the bones of the nose violently fractured.

The body has multiple bruises, burns and scratches, which could indicate that it was dragged, already dead, into the hedge. Examination also reveals several broken ribs, a fracture in the right tibia, lesions on both kneecaps, a haemorrhage in the right kidney and cranial trauma.

Death was probably caused by a heart attack following extensive torture.

Dr Robert Travis

When the telephone rang that morning it seemed a bit early to Ezima. But then she was dragged back to the breakfast table by the noise of the children: Tadjou's teenage moaning, Baïna nagging, Ima screaming, burnt toast, milk boiling over, all these cereals and jams she had never come across until a few weeks ago. As soon as Nwankwo reappeared in the kitchen doorway, she felt that something had changed, or rather that something had started again.

He didn't say anything, except to urge Tadjou to hurry up or else he would be late for his swimming lesson. He tried to conceal the excitement he had felt since Helen's call had come. He had gone outside to speak to her. According to information from Scotland Yard, governor Finley was going to be in London in a few days' time. His affairs had clearly suffered from the failure of a bank in the Faroe Islands, and he was hurrying over to sort things out. Helen had some information about his accounts, and she wanted to take advantage of the banking chaos to speak to him as part of the anti-laundering investigation. She wanted to see Nwankwo as soon as possible. Since hanging up, he felt a wave of excitement coursing through his body. He grabbed his car keys. Ezima came out of the kitchen, following him until they were face to face.

"What's going on?" She asked.

"Nothing, nothing at all. I'm just in a hurry, I don't want Tadjou to be late for his lesson, and—"

"What was that telephone call about?"

"Why all these questions?"

"Because I know you, Nwankwo. I don't know who rang, but I saw your face afterwards, and I know that look all too well."

"Listen—"

125

"No, you listen to me! Listen to your children laughing. Haven't you noticed that they're shouting and arguing out loud nowadays, even laughing louder – they're just so much more confident now. Back there at home they didn't dare, they were always scared, scared for you, for themselves, they kept quiet. Look at them now!"

"Ezima, it was the fraud squad. They want to speak to me. Finley is coming to London and they want to corner him. They need me to tell them what I know."

"So it's starting all over again."

"No! This time it's not me in the front line. It's the British in charge of the inquiry. And anyway this is a democratic country where... well, where we've got nothing to fear..."

He had been about to say "where they don't shoot people on street corners", but he'd thought of Lira and stopped in mid-sentence. In any case his wife was hardly listening.

"You're the one that scares me, not them..."

Tadjou appeared down the stairs, with his satchel on his back.

"Let's go!" Nwankwo said, his hand on his son's neck.

A few miles away, Lira was sitting up in her hospital bed. The bandage covered her face from her eyebrows to the bottom of her nose. Dmitry was beside her, talking gently, at random, trying to hide the distress and nausea he felt in this hospital. He was giving a lyrical description of the isolated house in the mountains where he had left their daughter. He described the fruit-laden trees in front of it, the young hikers who passed by whom Polina might befriend. He had in fact hardly seen anything. He had simply found out that his old friend had become a radical green, and had no telephone, TV, computer or electricity, and that he and his daughter would have to make arrangements to speak to each other at the telephone box in the village. He had stayed for less than an hour, just time to make some introductions, and then he had left Polina there on the path, angry and worried. He had been in a hurry to get to England.

"But who are these people, you never mentioned them?" Lira asked.

Dmitry told her about Jacques, the son of a French communist, who had learnt Russian at school and had come to Moscow thirty years ago. They had become friends and had then lost sight of each other. A few years later, Jacques, now a film designer, had looked him up in St Petersburg.

"What did you tell him about the situation?"

"The truth. Except for your eyes – you didn't want Polina to know."

"Yes, for her it would seem as if I were dead."

He had so often imagined himself having to rush to Lira's bedside, and so often imagined arriving too late. She had been playing with fire for so long, and he could not stop worrying about her despite the separation. Those who said he still loved her after three years were wrong. He certainly didn't expect her to come back to him, but he was still afraid for her, which was a different matter, even though that fear was a way of still being connected to her. He admired and resented her at the same time, would draw away and then explode with fury when he heard from her. He was a calm and rational maths teacher and she played havoc with his emotions. In the last three days his head had been boiling with lists and plans: write to Jacques, fetch Polina from Paris, drive her to the Cévennes, set off back, go to London... He could no longer remember his reaction when she had called him for help. He had shouted her name and thrown the telephone across the room.

"Everything will be all right. You'll get better," he said.

"Don't waste your energy, Dmitry. It was acid. They don't do things by halves."

"They didn't kill you. You must have more tests before we know anything. There are marvellous specialists in Moscow, you know."

"I'm not going back."

"What do you mean?"

"I'm not going back to Russia, I'm going to ask for asylum, something like that anyway… I don't want to live in fear of being killed at any moment."

"But it happened here."

"Over there they'll finish me off."

The nurse came in to change the dressing. Dmitry stood back, but not far – he wanted to see Lira's eyes. The last bandage came off, revealing shrunken eyelids and raw skin peppered with little blisters, and inside just a dark pupil. Lira could not see Dmitry's chin trembling like a child about to cry; he realized that she had lost more than her eyesight, her beauty had gone, those blue eyes that he had loved so much. He saw her again as he had seen her for the first time, coming into a bar near the university; it had been the beginning of summer and she had caught the sun. Her eyes shone out from her flushed cheeks; he couldn't stop staring, he even dropped his newspaper. All would be darkness from now on. Dmitry held on to the bedstead, and could think of nothing to say, so he suggested she get out of bed and try to walk over to the window. She agreed and got her long pale legs, which were covered in bruises, out from under the sheet. The nurse protested at first but the couple had already started so she joined them, taking Lira's arm.

"You're blinking, that's a good sign, it's the light!"

"Maybe…"

They were in front of the window.

"What can you see?"

"The sky is blue."

"Not really."

"Well it's not raining at least, I'd hear it!"

"That's true…" Dmitry sighed.

He made a face. Lira had already developed stratagems. As always she minimized any problem, especially with him. But the fact was she couldn't see anything. The sky was dark, it looked as though it might rain. They slowly went back to the bed. Lira lay down with a sigh that betrayed how exhausted she was by the effort she had just made. The nurse put on a new bandage. When she had gone, Dmitry returned to their conversation.

"Lira, you must come home."

"It's out of the question."

"You've got nobody here, no friends or relations, and you can't see!"

"A minute ago, you thought I would be able to see again."

"I still hope so. But whatever happens to your eyesight, you'll need help. I spoke to someone at the embassy, they want to help us. They'll arrange your travel, your treatment and legal help."

"They'll finish me off on the plane!"

"Look, that's enough with your caricatures and conspiracy theories. If you come home they'll leave you alone."

"I dare say you're right, now that I can't do anything... They'll probably give me a guide dog and a white stick!"

There was a sharp knock at the door. Nwankwo came in.

"Nwankwo!" Lira cried.

Dmitry was surprised by the warmth in her voice. So was she, but she sensed Nwankwo's energy and urgency – something important was happening, so different from all the hushed sighs of the others who were condemning her to a kind of limbo. She quickly sensed that the two men were uneasy with one another and she gently asked Dmitry if he wouldn't mind leaving them. He didn't flinch, and just bent over her, pulling up the sheet that was down over her thighs, and took her hands in his and kissed them.

"I'll come back this afternoon. Do you need anything?"

"No, I'm fine."

He went and Nwankwo approached.

"Have you got anything to tell me?" Lira pressed him.

"I've just come from the fraud squad. Your Louchsky and my Finley were laundering their money in the same bank and it's just gone bust!"

For a brief moment Lira imagined what she could have done with this information if she had been able to. She would have grabbed the telephone, demanded some space in her magazine, and had the usual row with Igor, her editor, about his legendary caution. But all she could do now was listen to Nwankwo, hanging on his every word: they were like flashes of light in the dark night in which she now dwelt. Nwankwo was unstoppable. He told her that Finley was expected in London in the next few days, that the fraud squad was determined to catch him and interrogate him, and that he would be on hand to give them a few discreet hints.

Lira's hand wandered up and down his forearm. He let her carry on, a little embarrassed – it was the gesture of a blind person, not that of a woman; she needed to feel him at her fingertips. She hadn't seen enough of him, or known him well enough, to be able to fully imagine him. Now she remembered his tall, thin, nervous body, with all that rage and energy barely contained in his teacher's suit. She could sense the nuances in his voice, which words came easily and which he had to search for. Lira's ear was working hard without her being conscious of it – her senses were adjusting to one another.

Nwankwo did her such a lot of good. If she could have drawn him it would have been with boxing gloves. She would be in the shadows behind him, like a coach or a fan, urging him on: "Go on, punch them! Do it for me!"

He was the only one still fighting.

It was rumoured in the law courts that the clerk had shouted at the judge when he reappeared the day after his disappearance, that he had called him names, called him a pathetic fool, a deserter, and that ever since that *lèse-majesté* they were no longer on speaking terms. The most knowledgeable claimed to know things about this curious team – the childless judge and his homosexual clerk. There's nothing gossips like better than disaster. However they are often ill-informed, and always behind the times. They could peer at the closed door of the judge's office, even listen at the door as much as they liked, they would still have been a long way from the truth of the matter.

The judge sat, frozen and pale, opposite Félix, hardly able to look up. The shouting and lies of the day after – "a friend in trouble" he had said, and Félix had not dared to contradict him – were already ancient history. The judge had just heard about Eyvin's death from his British counterparts.

"His body was found just outside London," he said. "It took a bit of time to identify the body. I know what you're thinking, Félix, and you're right."

Félix didn't ask about the condition in which Eyvin's body had been found, although he wanted to. He said nothing. He just stared at the empty chair opposite him, the chair in which the frightened young man with the childish mouth had sat asking for help. He heard himself say, thinking he was cleverer than the others, "this isn't the safest place". And, worst of all, he heard the voice on the telephone shouting "They're following me!" It was all he could think of, and it spurred him on.

"I'm leaving this evening," he said.

"Very good. I've signed for your leave of absence. I'll tell someone there that you're coming, it's safer. You may not be the only one who knows the address he gave you."

"No. Don't tell anyone."

"Well, at least keep me informed. I might be able to help."

"There's nothing the law courts can do."

"I know. But I can help you. We can pass information on to people better placed than us."

"Like who? The fraud squad? They're stuck, the public prosecutor is blocking everything."

"Well, it's up to you."

In the last few days, without anyone saying anything, there had been a kind of transfer of authority between them. They were no longer operating within a legal framework. There was a ghost sitting in the room with them, reproaching them for having done nothing to save him. The judge quietly returned to his desk and started work on a dossier, but going through the motions like an actor with a stage prop. Time went by in this strange atmosphere: there was so much to say, so much to try to understand – the drowned wife, the bankruptcy, the murdered interpreter, so many questions unanswered. But the answers would not come from within these walls.

Then Félix's telephone rang, with its silly tune. It was Do.

"Ah, the kamikaze! Sorry not to have rung back sooner. How are you? I'm in Nice as it happens. I'm in court this afternoon, if you're free for a drink. I'll meet you in the law courts."

"No, not in the court."

Félix gave him the address of a little restaurant he was fond of, which had Fifties-style lights in the ceiling, and then hung up. Suddenly the door opened, and Sergio the singer came in with his lawyer. He was nervous, his face sunburnt, and he seemed a great deal more upset than he had been on the day he had been interviewed about the death of his so-called great friend Linda Stephensen. He began talking before he had even sat down: he had been ruined by the failure of Grind Bank, he would lose everything, his villa in Saint-Tropez would be seized. He had borrowed fifteen million from a subsidiary of Grind Bank to do some work on it, with the house itself as guarantee, that was the way these things were done. He spoke fast, reeling off figures – forty per cent of the loan had been paid into his current account, and the rest into a life-insurance policy run by the Faroe Island bank…

"What's this got to do with us?" the judge interrupted.

The singer stopped and turned towards his lawyer. The lawyer expressed indignation at such lack of respect towards his client, beginning to raise his voice. The judge looked on with a weary expression that seemed to say "I've had enough of these overpaid self-important lawyers, enough of rich people mourning for their villas and not their friends, enough of everything."

"The death of the banker's wife, the bankruptcy, it's all connected, isn't it?" the lawyer snapped.

"Maybe, but the investigation is closed. The verdict was drowning."

"An investigation can be reopened!" the lawyer protested.

"Those people have stolen from me, they've abused me, taken everything," the singer went on.

"Just a week ago they were your best friends!" the judge retorted.

Félix sent a message from his computer: *Louchsky?*

"Let's get things straight," the judge continued. "Either you know something about the fraudulent goings on at the bank, which might have cost Mrs Stephensen her life, in which case you tell us about them, or you go elsewhere. Do you know Sergei Louchsky?"

"Are you implying that my client might have participated in illegal activities?"

"I'm simply saying that here we're dealing with dead bodies. Grind Bank going bust isn't my department."

"So what am I supposed to do? Just let myself be fleeced after a forty-year career?" Sergio shouted, getting up from his chair.

The mention of the forty-year career suddenly conjured up an image of all those terrible variety shows, those miserable Saturday nights in front of the television. It was all too much for Félix, who was feeling claustrophobic and was already late for his appointment with Do.

"You sang on the night the President was elected, didn't you?" he suddenly asked. "Why don't you go and talk to him about your problems?"

The singer and his lawyer were speechless. In any case the clerk had stopped transcribing anything. Protocol had gone out of the window and the judge couldn't help smiling. The visitors stormed out, no doubt feeding more rumours of rows and scenes. And then gloom descended once more. Félix grabbed his things and checked the time of his plane again. The judge stood up, held out his hand and held Félix's for a long time.

"Call me. Don't take any risks. Don't punish yourself, Félix."

As he ran to the restaurant, Félix realized that that had been the last interview they would do together. Do was waiting at the table when he came in. He greeted Félix drily, irritated at having had to wait so long and ill-pleased with the wine he had been given. He briskly called the waiter and ordered. Félix smiled.

"What's so funny?"

"You. You lawyers never stop arguing even when you're ordering a cup of coffee."

Do didn't rise to this – he was in a hurry, and went straight to the point.

"Listen, Félix, I've just got one thing to say to you: forget it. In five or ten years your friend Louchsky will own a television station and he'll be financing the next president of the Republic."

"You always think big!"

"And it hasn't done me any harm either…"

Félix should have agreed, but he kept quiet.

"Seriously," Do continued, "just look at his advisory board. A German ex-chancellor, an ex-head of the European Bank, and that's just the official ones. I'm sure our ex-president is involved as well. But don't spread that around, you know how money is reviled in this country…"

"They're all just has-beens."

"Listen to this young fool – no respect for his elders. Louchsky's story started a long time ago, twenty years back. At that time Russia was breaking into pieces, everything was for sale, and vultures were flying in from all over the world. Louchsky was very young then but he had already started climbing the ladder. That was when he met what's-her-name, the tall woman with the earrings – Vuipert, she was known as the Viper. She was working for a bank at the time, finding new markets; she and Louchsky got cosy. And now she's the President's special adviser."

"I see. Now I understand why the reaction was so quick."

"You haven't got a hope in hell! Your judge should have been a bit more subtle. He should have waited, started some peripheral investigations, I don't know. Was he trying to self-destruct or what?"

"What do we know about this character?"

"About him, nothing. If it's a choice between Louchsky or the Chinese, everybody prefers the Russian. Europe stretching from the Atlantic to the Urals. I can understand that. He's made a clean sweep of the world Monopoly board. There's hardly a takeover bid, a merger or a project that doesn't have his name attached. So eat up your salad, go on holiday and forget about it."

"I want it known that the judge was ruined after searching his villa."

"You may have done your utmost to disappoint your parents, Félix, you're still an arrogant little bourgeois. What did you find there?"

"Two guns, a fake Monet—"

"Forget about the paintings! Copies suit everybody, particularly insurance companies. I learnt that at the Ministry."

Félix was now in a hurry to get this over with. The flamboyant Do was no more than an establishment figure, saved a little by his gay mannerisms. He longed to go, to escape from all this cynicism. He would go to the address Eyvin had given him; he would spend the night with Mark who had texted him "Glad you're coming". That was all that mattered now.

They left the restaurant half an hour later. Félix went home to pack. He hesitated, looking at the envelopes full of photocopies of the dossier, and then pushed them into the bottom of his suitcase.

At the airport, with the sound of the loudspeakers in the background, Steffy called. He had probably been warned by Do that Félix was still playing the hero.

"Just want to see if everything's OK."

"You just want to see if the law is going to keep quiet!"

"Don't be like that. I'm worried about you. Louchsky's absolutely furious! He's throwing a party at Versailles next month for his fortieth birthday, and there's a big contract looming that I can't tell you about. So your little expedition to his villa and the failure of the bank have left him foaming. I'm saying it again, Félix, dive for cover. The dogs are out."

"What's the contract?"

"I just said, I can't tell you, I'm just warning you. It sounds as though you're at the airport."

"Yeah," Félix said, annoyed at being pinned down.

"Are you going to see Mark?"

"Yes, I need some air. I need him."

"Good, I'm glad you're getting together again. Just get away from all this, think of yourself, Félix. We all know you're too clever to be a mere clerk. But don't do anything stupid."

Once he was in the plane, stuck in a middle seat, Félix unfolded the *Guardian*, which he had picked up on boarding. He went straight to the financial pages: they were filled with stories about the failure of Grind Bank and the panic spreading among the big financial players in London. Eyvin's death was not mentioned, it obviously hadn't been made public yet. So Félix thought that perhaps he had not come too late, that he might yet find something or someone at the address, which he had wiped from his mobile and learnt by heart. He then idly turned to the news pages. He thought about Mark and began to believe in love again. Then he thought of Eyvin, and wondered whether he too might be killed. Just as he was brooding about life and death the air hostess began her safety demonstration.

His eye was suddenly caught by a headline at the bottom of the page: "Inquest on attack on Russian journalist Lira Kazan has stalled". And so Félix learnt that she was now blind. And she was in London.

III

SEPTEMBER

The plane landed in the area reserved for private jets, well away from the crowds, barriers, customs and formalities. A man got out. He had a leather briefcase with brass locks discreetly attached to his wrist by a chain. He had come from Nigeria. His chauffeur was waiting for him at the other side of the hangar, standing to attention, ready to murmur "This way, Governor" and open the rear door of the armoured Maybach limousine. But then three men interposed themselves.

"Mr Finley? Police," one of them said.

Finley's eyes were hidden behind dark glasses. He remained upright and haughty. The only sign of nerves was a tightening of his hand on the briefcase as the agents explained that they had a warrant to take him to the headquarters of the Serious Fraud Office, where he would be questioned. He appeared to consent, and undid the chain around his wrist so as to hand the briefcase to his colossus of a bodyguard.

"Sorry," the policeman said. "We'll take that. Customs."

Finley stepped backwards. He tried again to hand the briefcase to the bodyguard, with the contempt of somebody who felt untouchable.

"Put down that briefcase!"

Surprised, Finley obeyed. Everything then happened fast. The briefcase was seized, and the governor stepped into the car, in a cold rage. He knew that his assistant would already be calling his lawyers. They would go into action immediately and get him out of this. He just needed to be patient.

All this time, back at the headquarters of the Serious Fraud Office, Helen and Nwankwo were going over the final details.

"You must not come out of this room. You'll be able to see and hear everything that is said. It's all filmed, that's the law. You can even suggest lines of questioning over the intranet. You can be my prompter. But at no time must the governor see you, otherwise I'll be in serious trouble."

Helen was a small woman, who looked frail and nervous in her severe suit decorated with coloured brooches, but she did not lack authority and intuition. Her position was normally filled by ambitious, self-interested people. Helen was the exception and she knew it. She had risen almost invisibly through the ranks and had learnt a great deal along the way, more than she should have. And so when the collapse of Grind Bank was officially announced, she spotted a small window of opportunity. A very small one, but it was worth exploiting. A message appeared on her mobile.

"They'll be here in a quarter of an hour."

Nwankwo stiffened. Helen put a hand on his shoulder and repeated the conditions of their collaboration.

"Nwankwo, I can't perform miracles. His lawyer will arrive within the hour, and alarm bells will start ringing in high places. We haven't got much time. It's all going to be painful and frustrating for you, but you must promise me you'll stay out of it."

"I promise."

Helen shut the door.

Nwankwo watched from the window as Finley got out of the car. It was both pleasant and painful to see him escorted by two policemen, looking small down at the bottom of the building, the same man who had swaggered like a king into his Abuja office, and who had ordered the death of Uche as though he were crushing an insect. Ten minutes later, watching and listening to the interview taking place on the other side of the corridor, he felt choked once again by the power and arrogance of his enemy. Nwankwo clutched the edge of the table until his fingers were white.

Finley looked Helen up and down. He was one of those men who felt that a woman should automatically feel threatened by him. But Helen held his stare. She remained calm, asked him to be seated and state his identity, and to explain the reason for his visit to England. And then to open the briefcase.

"Certainly not!"

"I don't want to use any more force."

"Especially as it could backfire against you," replied Finley, his legs crossed and his chin held high in defiant certainty.

Helen remained impassive.

"Open it," Nwankwo muttered, alone in his room. "Open that fucking case!"

Helen ordered the guards to force the locks. The case was full of money.

"I hope you weren't planning to deposit this at Grind Bank!" she snarled. She was closing in. "Although according to my information you've got other accounts here in London."

She seemed to be stroking the dossier in front of her.

"This is not my money," the governor replied in a blank tone.

"Whose is it then?"

"I work for my country, madam, and I must sometimes remain silent. Your action, I repeat, is going to get you into serious trouble. Let's stop this little game now and nothing more will happen."

In his room, Nwankwo was sitting on the floor, leaning against the wall, with his papers spread around him. It was like playing a video game, conducting an interrogation without the accused before him and without Uche at his side. He wrote: *An 800-million-dollar contract was signed last month for the development of a new oilfield off the Nigerian coast. This must be his commission!*

The message appeared on Helen's screen. She glanced at it and continued with her questions.

"Mr Finley, according to our sources, a governor in Nigeria earns twenty-five thousand dollars a year. You have just bought a house in Hampstead for fifteen million pounds. Can you explain this?"

Finley shrugged, not bothering to reply.

"Mr Finley, I must ask you again. If, as we have been told, a Nigerian governor earns twenty-five thousand dollars a year, how were you able last year to buy a Bombardier jet for twenty million dollars – I have the proof of the sale on one of your bank accounts."

She carried on asking more and more questions, more and more sharply. Nwankwo was writing faster and faster, listing everything – the Jaguar, the Bentley, the mistress's flat, the tailors' bills. Behind every bill, behind every luxury brand, lay the misery of his country. Nwankwo was in a state of febrile excitement, with dilated pupils and shaking hands. Never before had any Nigerian official had to answer such questions about his lifestyle and his thefts. What he had not been able to achieve in his own country was happening here. *Look Uche, look at Finley shaking!* It was true, the governor's bravado had melted away, he was stammering, cursing, threatening: he realized that his whole life had been patiently laid bare, as though the British authorities had been watching him for many years.

And then the telephone rang on Helen's desk.

Nwankwo soon understood what was happening, if only because of the way she wasn't being allowed to finish her sentences. Without even hearing he knew who was talking and what was being said. They all said the same things: "Do you want to cause chaos in the City?" or "Some things can't be sorted out in an inspector's office!" And then Helen, putting down the receiver, said in a dignified but flat voice, and in the name of order, of the wider interests of the country's petrol or car companies and that of Her Majesty's Government:

"Mr Finley, our interview is over."

* * *

Nwankwo closed his eyes. He could hear the sound of the chair scraping, the briefcase being closed and, worst of all, Finley's triumphant sneering laugh. He rose from his chair and stood for a moment, his arms hanging at his side, momentarily lost in this room stuffed with useless evidence. He was shaking with rage now, he didn't know where to look. Devoured by his sense of helplessness he began to punch the wall. He felt no pain. He had become a human bombshell. Then he opened the door and went out. Finley was still there, still sniggering. Nwankwo charged towards him before the policemen understood what was happening. He grabbed the governor and held him against the wall by the neck, spitting in his face. He yelled that he would avenge Uche, that he would get him in the end… The police were finally able to drag him off and hold him down, with Helen looking on furiously. Nwankwo was still yelling.

Finley wiped his face. He went over to Nwankwo who was still being held down and whispered:

"But surely you know very well what happens to those who disrespect me."

He was admitting Uche's murder, and threatening another one. He went away, his head held much too high. The policemen released Nwankwo. Helen's door slammed. Nwankwo knocked on it three times.

"Get out!" she yelled from inside the room.

Nwankwo remained frozen in the corridor. He had to go now. He would never come back. He went back into the little room where he had been listening to the interview and laboriously gathered up his documents. He was still driven by an unstoppable rage, by images that wouldn't go away. He had been humiliated too often to respect procedures that no longer concerned him, and, without premeditation, he turned off the light, closed the door, inserted his USB memory stick into the computer and transferred the film of the interview onto it. The corridor was now silent, the calm after the storm. The copying took several minutes. Then he crept away, his heart beating as though he were a thief.

When he got home, all was quiet. Even the little one didn't jump into his arms. The children watched him go past the sofa and up the stairs. Children sense things about their parents, when they are angry, when they love each other, when they are trying to conceal something. They could hear their mother's strangled voice upstairs.

"They'll deport us!" Ezima was saying.

"No, I'm sure they won't do that."

Nwankwo was lying, he was no longer sure of anything. Helen might forgive him for his outburst, his shouting, even the violent attack, because she knew what he had been through, but she would never forgive him for taking the film, and he was determined to make use of it.

"School starts in three days. The children are dreading it, they don't know anyone here, they'll be the little new ones, and…"

"…and the little blacks, I know."

"So?"

"So, I love you and I'm just bringing you bad luck. But I feel as though I'm carrying Uche on my back, you see. Wherever I go, I'm carrying him. I won't put him down until Finley has got what he deserves."

"On your back? That's where your children should be! They're alive, Uche's dead!"

"I wouldn't wish anyone to know what I know or to see what I've seen. It's unbearable. I've tried, Ezima, but I am no longer capable of living a normal life."

"What are you saying?"

"That for the moment you should put your name down instead of mine at the children's school. And that I should go and sleep somewhere else for the time being."

"All this means is that it's even worse here than it was there," Ezima sighed.

Libération, 4th September 2010

The President's lunch guest today was pretty discreet for a Russian oligarch. Serge Louchsky, said to be the richest man in his country, has been buffeted in the last few years by a series of financial crises. He is investing more and more heavily in France, where he already owns a villa on Cap Ferrat and a luxurious apartment in Paris. According to the spokesman for the Élysée, speaking to Agence France-Presse: "You cannot promote your country's financial interests without meeting businessmen. And sometimes you sympathize more with some than others, the ones who have some vision for the future. In a new world, you need new ideas and new men..."

What could Eyvin possibly have left in a place like this? Félix wondered as he stood at the foot of tower block L. He dragged his feet along, his stomach in knots and his lips tight – he knew the address by heart, *Caliban Towers, Block L, top floor, Steve.* He gazed up at the windows dotted with satellite dishes, the youths sitting on the steps, killing time if nothing else, and the pubescent graffiti all over the walls of the hall and lift. What could the young blond prodigy, snapped up by the bank, possibly have left in such a place?

Félix pressed the button for the fourteenth floor, and the lift doors closed. It took off, with Félix as pale as if he were going into outer space. Top floor. Steve had written his first name on the bell, and had left a pair of muddy trainers outside the door. You could hear his music from the stairwell. Eyvin's secret friend didn't appear to be very threatening so far. Perhaps he was a childhood friend. Félix rang twice.

"Who's there?" a slightly hoarse voice called.

Félix stammered out his name. The door opened on an extremely scruffy young man.

"Eyvin gave me this address," Félix said.

"Eyvin's dead."

"I know and I'm afraid that's why I'm here. He left something for me."

Steve beckoned him in, shut the door, and leaving him standing in the hall went off to dig around among his CDs. There were great heaps of them, decades of music, which went well with the rows of empty beer bottles arranged around the kitchen floor. The flat smelt of permanent adolescence, a life completely opposite to Eyvin's banker's existence. Steve came back with two CDs in boxes labelled with British groups Félix had never heard of. He took them, not asking what was in them. But he certainly knew more than Steve who gently pushed him out of the door.

"I'm sorry, but I don't want you to stay here."

"I understand. Were you friends for long?"

"We shared rooms for six months at the beginning of university. He called me a month ago, I hadn't heard from him for a year. He blew in, left the discs and went off again. Then he texted me your name and that's all."

When Steve had heard about his death he had done nothing, moved nothing in his flat. He hadn't sought to understand or to protect himself. "It's a shit world," was all he said.

There was a sweet smell of limes coming from the flat opposite. The half-open door revealed a neat interior with tablecloths and paper flowers. Félix nodded his agreement; yes, it was a shit world. He suddenly felt like some kind of stain on this landing. He had to go and leave Steve to his electric guitars, and the African family to cook their dinner. He must take Eyvin's CDs with all the secrets and crimes they contained far away from these people's simple lives and just leave them in peace. He said goodbye and set off down the stairs, ignoring the lift, with, in his pocket, the musicless CDs.

Back at Mark's, Félix settled down in front of the computer. Six years of bank statements unfurled beneath his eyes. There were dates, debits, credits, strings of noughts like a row of bubbles. Millions, billions of dollars moving around the world. The crazy growth of Grind Bank was re-enacted before his eyes. And now it was foundering in the icy waters of the Faroe Islands. Félix became drunk on the figures. He had never had such a document at his fingertips before. It was a complete confession. All the gaps were filled in. This was the holy grail for any investigator: the pieces of the puzzle began to fit together, dark corners were lit up. He plunged into it, trying to decipher every line, cross-checking them with the documents he had brought from Nice, the notes taken from Louchsky's house, Linda Stephensen's bank statements. He lost all sense of time. Eyvin had died under torture, without talking, for the sake of these documents. Félix wanted to be worthy of him. There was one thing he was sure of: the men who had killed him were the same as those who had attacked Lira. He must find her.

The judge rang at the appointed time and, as agreed, asked vague questions, to which Félix gave anodyne answers that his superior could decode. They were quite sure they were being listened to. "The flapping ears are at work," the judge used to say without knowing that one day they would be listening to him. They invented words, images, codes, like schoolboys, without realizing that they had now gone over to the other side – they were now the pursued, not the pursuers. When Félix said the tailor's address he had been given had been brilliant, the judge understood that Eyvin had left behind a bombshell.

"Well, take care not to get soaked. Don't go out without your umbrella."

Mark came home, dressed as usual with sober elegance. He stroked the back of Félix's neck, talking to him in the way he used to: "You OK, old fellow?" He wanted a drink and went to get one for Félix as well. Félix turned off his computer. Mark knew that he was looking for Lira, but not that his flat was now full of explosive documents. Félix watched him, listened to him cursing and laughing about his day, the delays at the building site and so on. He wanted to let himself be enveloped by the atmosphere of this splendid apartment. Their reunion had gone well the night before and there had been no grand explanations. Love seemed possible once again. But Félix found himself incapable of taking advantage of the situation. He was completely immersed in these figures and obsessed with all these secrets.

"I'll take you to see some Russians this evening. Who knows, she might be there," Mark said. Félix didn't know if he was joking or if he had already had enough of hearing about this Lira.

An hour later they went into the reception rooms of one of the big hotels on Hyde Park that was frequented by powerful Russians and their entourage of admirers and confidants. All the talk was of country houses, salerooms, smart restaurants and the best schools for their children. Mark felt quite at home. He had only arrived two months earlier but had already adapted himself to the customs and language of the high-earning London expat community – even to the extent of pouring scorn on the fuddy-duddy French. He found a table and ordered two vodkas. Félix only half-listened as he told him about the latest developments on his building site. The drinks came.

"You know what these are called?" said a man at a neighbouring table, pointing at their glasses.

"No."

"Putins!"

They all laughed. Félix looked around him. There were a few rich Arabs mingling with the Russians, and a fire blazed in the hearth even though it was still mild outdoors, but everything here was done for the sake of the decor. These prosperous men with their designer-clad wives had come to London for business and financial reasons, but also in order to enjoy a romantic splendour that had never been tainted by revolution. Félix watched these caviar immigrants, as they were known; Lira would not have been at home here, he was sure. He imagined her as a quite different type, more like an energetic terrier. Where could she possibly be? Mark, still deep in conversation with the vodka-drinker, nudged him. Félix started listening to them.

"Louchsky's the most secretive and busy of the lot. Everybody is amazed at how fast he's rising," the friendly neighbour was saying. "Look, over there, that's someone who knows him well, his lawyer – mine too – he's called Jonas Rassmussen."

The name rang a bell in Félix's mind. He watched the man working the room. He seemed to know everybody. He probably acted for them all. He had a hard face and jaw, and the toned body of somebody who worked up a sweat every day in a top-of-the-range gym. Félix knew he had seen that name, maybe in one of the card indexes, perhaps a payment by Louchsky to his lawyer. Or had he seen it earlier, in one of the dossiers?… Then he remembered: the logbook. The man had been on board the Stephensen yacht, several times. He was approaching them. He came up and greeted the neighbour, his client. Félix pressed his fingers together, signalling to Mark to keep his mouth shut. Rassmussen must have sensed their stares – he looked at them long enough for the neighbour to introduce them, as two visiting Frenchmen.

"Where are you from in France?" Rassmussen asked, in French.

"Nice," said Mark.

"What an idiot," Félix thought. Next thing you knew he would be telling them that he worked at the law courts.

However Rassmussen seemed to think they were staying in the hotel, which would certainly exclude them from being mere civil servants, and then his phone vibrated, summoning him back to business. Félix was relieved to see him go. He could still feel the man's penetrating, all-seeing stare – this man who must at this very moment be frantically searching for what Félix had in his possession.

University College Hospital
Night Report
7th September

Room 24

30mg morphine administered at 1.00 a.m. to patient Lira Kazan.
She had become delirious in her sleep, agitated, trying to remove
her bandages, shouting and confused.

He could still see the same car in his rear-view mirror. And he could feel Baïna still kicking the back of his seat, swinging her short legs, reminding him that he still had children and that school had just finished. He must force himself to listen to all the names of her new school friends, and try to remember them; he must buy such and such a satchel, and a special kind of pencil – she wanted to have the same things as the others... He had to put out of his mind, just for a moment, the thought of Lira lying on her hospital bed refusing to go home to her country, suspicious that her husband was secretly organizing her return, afraid, desperate to carry on with her work. He must forget Helen – she could probably do something for Lira, but she no longer answered his calls.

Baïna was still talking. Nwankwo smiled, agreeing to all her demands. He looked again at the car behind them and then, still in the mirror, at his eight-year-old daughter with her bright and cheerful little face and her African braids, specially done for her first day at school. She hadn't asked him why he was no longer sleeping at home. On the first evening she had just said: "It's because of Uche, isn't it?" Her big brother had just sighed, now as silent as the grown-ups, and the little one hadn't reacted at all. Nwankwo hadn't denied it. He knew that when he arrived at the house he would kiss the children, spend a few moments alone in the kitchen with Ezima – they were neither together nor apart, they were just nowhere – and then leave. He was living with his colleague Julian Bolton. He had asked him to suggest a hotel the day after the interrogation in Helen's office. Bolton had said that he had a spare room with a bathroom, that he was divorced and diabetic and would appreciate the

157

company and didn't mind the risk. Nwankwo had refused at first and had spent two nights in a hotel; then he relented, bowing to friendship despite the possible danger. He had even thought that perhaps Lira could come and stay there for a while.

He was becoming fed up with this car on his heels – it was beginning to scare him. He saw a service station and turned in. He didn't need petrol but it would be a way of finding out if he were really being followed. The other car carried on past. It had been a false alarm. They set off again ten minutes later, Baïna armed now with a noisy packet of sweets.

They hadn't gone more than a quarter of a mile when Nwankwo recognized the same car, now coming towards them. A man on the back seat was pulling out a gun. Nwankwo swerved onto the verge, off the crowded road; he hooted and accelerated, shouting: "Get down, Baïna! Get onto the floor!"

The first shot shattered the back window. "Baïna!" Nwankwo screamed, but the little girl didn't answer. The second shot hit the bodywork. "Baïna, speak to me! Don't move, just say something!" Nwankwo begged, still driving. If he stopped the others would too, and they would then be shot down like rabbits. Nwankwo had no gun.

"Say something, baby, speak to me!" he shouted, putting his right hand back between the seats. He looked around quickly. Baïna was like a little rigid ball, not moving. He stroked her hair – "Say something, Baïna" – and eventually he heard a few stifled moans. She was alive!

He turned left and drove on, still stroking his daughter, dreading seeing blood on his fingers. When he thought he had gone far enough he drew up. He rushed around to the back, taking Baïna's face between his hands. Her eyes were open, her lips trembling. She had pieces of glass in her curly hair. She had clearly not been hit. He pulled her out and lifted her up, wrapping her legs around him; he put her head on his shoulder with his large hand over it and went back to sit with her on the driver's seat.

He sat there for several minutes without moving, Baïna huddled against him, saying it was OK for her to cry, that it was normal – she had been scared and so had he and he loved her so much. In the end he was the one who cried, his streaming eyes reflected in the mirror in which he was still looking out for his assassins.

US EMBASSY, COPENHAGEN

CONFIDENTIAL

SECTION 01.081657

SEPTEMBER 10

SUBJECT: FAILURE OF GRIND BANK. MEETING BETWEEN AMBASSADOR AND SUNLEIF STEPHENSEN.

MEETING BETWEEN AMBASSADOR, COMMERCIAL ATTACHÉ AND BANKER SUNLEIF STEPHENSEN, RECENTLY DECLARED BANKRUPT. HE WAS ASKED TO CLARIFY HIS CONNECTION WITH SERGEI LOUCHSKY. HE WAS UNWILLING TO SPEAK BUT DID NOT DENY ANYTHING WHEN IT WAS SUGGESTED THAT GRIND BANK HAD BEEN USED TO LAUNDER RUSSIAN MONEY. HE CLAIMED NOT TO HAVE ORIGINALLY UNDERSTOOD THE FRAUDULENT NATURE OF CERTAIN TRANSACTIONS.

STEPHENSEN IS A ROUGH TYPE, SHARP BUT EXTREMELY IMPRESSIONABLE. HE IS NOT A MARKET SPECIALIST AND HE DOES NOT SPEAK LIKE A TYPICAL BANKER. HE SAYS THAT HE FEARS FOR HIS LIFE. HIS WIFE DIED IN SUSPICIOUS CIRCUMSTANCES IN FRANCE. THE BODY OF HIS PERSONAL ASSISTANT HAS BEEN FOUND, BADLY MUTILATED, A SHORT DISTANCE OUTSIDE LONDON. ACCORDING TO THE DANISH PRESS ALL THE BANK'S RECORDS WERE DESTROYED JUST BEFORE THE RECEIVERS WERE CALLED IN. ONLY A CONFESSION AND DETAILED EXPLANATIONS FROM SUNLEIF STEPHENSEN CAN BACK UP OUR SUSPICIONS AND JUSTIFY A REVOCATION OF SERGEI LOUCHSKY'S US VISA.

AS AGREED WE HAVE OFFERED HIM PROTECTION IN EXCHANGE
FOR INFORMATION. HE SAID THAT HE NEEDED TO THINK
ABOUT IT BUT HE SEEMED INTERESTED IN THE IDEA. HE
AGREED TO MEET AGAIN HERE IN A FEW DAYS' TIME.

It seemed to all of them that Ima hadn't stopped crying once since they had left Lagos, climbing down that ladder at the port. It wasn't true – she was crying today, yes, but that was all right, she was crying because she had to leave her doll's house behind. She hadn't cried about all the other things; she had wanted to, but she hadn't dared to; she had learnt to stop herself. She hadn't cried about the cupboards hastily emptied out, the comings and goings, Ezima swearing that she wouldn't remain a second longer, screaming that they had almost killed her daughter, Tadjou the big brother trying to be the man of the family, Baïna lying on the sofa repeating that there was nothing wrong, she hadn't been that frightened, she didn't want to leave her father. And her father, who had become the onlooker to his family's fate, the cause of it even, was there too, clumsily helping them with their departure. No she hadn't cried about all that. She had wanted to, but she had learnt not to.

When Nwankwo and Baïna had come back from the hospital after the accident, Ezima had been on the doorstep. She had hugged her daughter, but not for long. She had pushed Nwankwo out of the house, banging her fists against his chest, taking no notice of the children, the neighbours or the two policemen who were escorting them. She screamed that he was no longer a father or a husband, he was just a madman. He let her scream for a moment and then grabbed her wrists firmly and in silence, just to calm her down. Ima had watched, without crying.

The tears had come when it was time to say goodbye to her father and get into a police car which was going to take them to a cousin she didn't know in London. Ima thought about her doll's house with its miniature plates on the table, the miniature flowery pillowcases on the bed, the miniature version of happiness inside, and then she cried. Leaving that behind, that was why she was crying, whatever the others might say. They didn't realize that she was a big girl now, and that she had kept quiet for weeks. They still thought she hadn't stopped crying since leaving Lagos, climbing down that ladder at the port. The fact was they needed her to be crying – she had to cry for everybody.

Nwankwo gave a great sigh; the air he breathed in seemed to scorch his lungs. He was burning up inside. It was better that they should go. He hadn't known what to say, he had just tried to express himself with his hands, big hands made to hold children. Baïna was fine, that was what mattered, but that was no argument, she could have died that day. So could he of course, but that was in the nature of things, to be expected almost.

The next day Nwankwo found the two protection officers waiting outside his door. He knew how to live with this type of escort. They weren't planning to keep it up for long – he wasn't an official person, just a teacher living in exile. He greeted them and walked along to the criminology department. There, amid the excitement of a new term starting, people turned to look at him, and it was clear from the lowered eyes and the over-sympathetic greetings that news of the attack had spread. He was told in the secretary's office that he could have three weeks' leave. He replied that he didn't need it, that he was keen to start work, but they eventually made it clear that it would be necessary for the students' safety as well. He set off down the corridors in search of Bolton to tell him that he wouldn't stay any longer. He could have his house back to himself again. He didn't want to expose anyone else to any danger. As he approached the staffroom he overheard an excited conversation between three lecturers about the previous day's incident.

"Fancy having cops in the classroom!"

"And for someone like him! In the end he's no safer here than back at home!"

"The students will be thrilled."

"And we're going to look like fools with our comparative-criminality courses."

"Old fools you mean. We can't compete with a teacher who's been shot at the day before with his little girl on the back seat."

"Especially as we're all beyond the school-run stage of life."

Nwankwo wrote a note for Bolton, left it at the reception desk and fetched his car again. He drove to London, his escorts still with him. He was secretly hoping for a message from Helen, thinking that perhaps news of the attack would calm her fury, but she didn't call. Two hours later, he was at the hospital. In the corridor he could hear shouts coming from Lira's room. He recognized one of them as Dmitry. He was speaking Russian, and laying down the law. There was a woman too, waiting outside. She seemed to be hesitating about going in. Nwankwo slowed down. Perhaps this wasn't such a good idea.

"Mr Ganbo?" the woman said.

"Yes."

"I'm Charlotte MacKennedy. I'm a friend of Lira's. I work at the *Guardian*."

"Oh yes, I read your piece, in fact I'm here thanks to you."

"Well it's thanks to me that she went to see you. I suggested it. I had heard about your arrival in Oxford."

"I sent her packing," Nwankwo admitted, lowering his head. "What's happening? Does he want her to go home?"

"Yes he's organized her repatriation for tomorrow. The doctor has signed a release. But she doesn't want to go."

The door opened and Dmitry appeared. When he saw Nwankwo he seemed to freeze. He hesitated and then came over.

"If you've got the slightest affection or respect for her, you'd do well not to give her any bad ideas."

"She's strong – much too strong to let herself be influenced."

"What matters today isn't whether she's strong or weak, it's whether she lives or dies!"

He turned on his heels. Charlotte and Nwankwo watched him go without reproaching him. They shared his sense of powerlessness. They went into the room. Lira seemed to be expecting them. She sat on the edge of the bed, with her legs dangling a few inches off the ground. Even those few inches seemed to give her vertigo, and that vertigo had become the justification for looking after her, for things to be decided for her by a husband she had left years earlier, in the offices of an embassy which regarded her as an enemy.

She moved her head, said no and again no. If she had been dead anyone could have taken her body, even those who had intended to kill her. But she was alive, very much alive, and was still capable of deciding about what would happen to her. She felt herself to be a dead weight, not just to herself but to others; everything was dark inside her as well as outside – in her head, her mouth, words came out with difficulty as though afraid to be heard. It was all so painful, but in the end she forced herself to say:

"Could anyone have me to stay for a while, just to give me time to get organized?"

"There's room in my house," Nwankwo said at once.

He added:

"But I must warn you, it won't be particularly safe. I've got a few killers after me too."

Lira knew nothing about the attempted murder of the day before and she didn't ask any questions. She was delighted – a decision had been taken, a risky one certainly, but her own. As agreed, when Dmitry came back that afternoon, she kept quiet. And when he reminded her of the timetable for the following day, eleven o'clock departure by ambulance for the airport and a two o'clock flight to St Petersburg, she continued to protest, but weakly. He became gentler, and seemed to believe that she had resigned herself to her fate. After all, what choice did she have now? He had hardly left when Charlotte reappeared. She had brought some clothes for Lira. She helped her get dressed, insisting on tying a scarf around her head. Lira laughed softly.

"There's nothing to worry about! They think I'm going to catch their wretched plane tomorrow? What on earth are you making me look like?"

"Marianne Faithfull escaping from her fans, thirty years ago!"

There was hardly anything to take with them from the room, just the medicines and lotions prescribed by the doctor. Lira had no possessions of her own. Then they left, saying goodbye to the nurse, who assumed everything was in order since the release had been signed. Lira felt Charlotte's arm trembling with fear. Nwankwo was waiting in the car park. He opened the door. Lira lingered for a moment; it was so long since she had felt fresh air on her face. Charlotte hugged her before she got in:

"I wish I could have done more," she said.

"Don't worry, this will be fine." Nwankwo closed the car door.

"Charlotte, thank you for everything, I'll keep you posted. Don't call me. I'll ring."

And they set off. In his rear-view mirror now there were two policemen whose job it was to protect him. They would protect her too, he thought.

He would write her a note, but since Lira could no longer read, it would have to be one that could be read out to her, not saying too much... Félix approached the entrance to University College Hospital, where he had read that she was, wondering how he would get past the barriers in order to speak to her. His reflection in the glass doors still seemed to wobble: Mark had dragged him to a nightclub the evening before. It had been one of those wild noisy bars, full of men, with alcoves for assignations between people escaping from their conventional daytime existence. They had got home at dawn, still far from sober. At least the hospital's reply had been clear: Lira Kazan was no longer there, the woman said, not even looking at the file. Félix only had one card left: the journalist who had written the article. "Kings Place, 90 York Way," he told the taxi driver.

"Charlotte MacKennedy? She's not available," the receptionist said. She was a tiny, heavily made-up girl sitting in the middle of a huge, light-filled hall with *The Guardian – The Observer* etched in giant letters on the glass partitions. She hadn't said Charlotte was absent, so Félix indicated that he would wait. He stood around, pretending to be interested in the photographs exhibited in the entrance, and the television screens from which world events seemed to spew like volcanic lava – they were the only indication that this was a place that dealt in news and current affairs. Otherwise this clean, modern, smooth building could have been that of any random insurance company. A tide of journalists came in and out, talking fast. Félix remembered his adolescent years listening to the BBC with gratitude. Nothing escaped him. He stood there for an hour, maybe two, feeling that he had become invisible. A man and a woman came down the escalator, arguing.

"We can't print that statement!" she said.

"We're cornered," he answered.

"It's a pack of lies!"

"Rassmussen is dangerous, Charlotte, he won't let go. And I don't want to have to pay damages and costs to Louchsky."

Rassmussen, Louchsky, Charlotte! The winning combination! The words he heard made Félix wonder if he might still be under the effect of the hallucinogenic drugs of the night before.

The two figures left the building. Félix fell in behind them. They were walking fast, Charlotte in very high heels. Félix could no longer hear what they were saying, and waited for them to separate, but they went into a restaurant together. It was lunchtime. Félix chose not to follow them in, but bought a sandwich and a newspaper and settled on a bench within sight of the restaurant door. He felt like a private detective on an assignment. He hardly looked up at this development surrounded by water. The canal and the boats reminded him of a barge that he had seen in a documentary on television about the City of London: a priest on board heard confessions during the lunch hour. Traders could be forgiven for all the harm they had done to the world in the time it took to eat a sandwich. It was a pity they couldn't tape the confessions, Félix thought, as Linda Stephensen's shrink had done. That would have been a fascinating research project all right – hearing about the complexes of those who dealt in everything and nothing. He sometimes remembered what she had said; it came to him in entire sentences, nothing that advanced the inquiry, just enough to glimpse the chaos of a muddled life:

"When I got married, my father, who was a doctor, couldn't stop saying: 'This is the most successful operation of my life!' I was marrying the richest man on the island!"

Félix wouldn't have liked Linda Stephensen alive, but now she was dead he was becoming rather fond of her.

Finally the couple reappeared and went their separate ways. Charlotte MacKennedy took out her mobile. This wasn't the moment to approach her. She went into a supermarket. Odd, that habit women have of always wanting to do some shopping just after lunch. In the household aisle she picked up soap, face cream, shampoo, cotton wool, hairbands and a hairbrush. She was filling up a basket – she seemed to be re-equipping her entire bathroom. Félix was just about to go up to her, but hesitated, trying to order what he wanted to say to her. Now she went to the underwear section. He might start looking suspicious if he began hovering around alone among the knickers. She chose plain cotton ones, some white and some black, without lace. Félix thought she would have worn more exotic lingerie, which would have gone better with her painted nails and high-heeled shoes. He grabbed some aftershave and stood behind her at the checkout. It was his last chance – she would be out in the street, on the telephone again and back in the office if he didn't speak now. "Excuse me, miss, I need to speak to you about Lira Kazan. It's urgent, I've got something for her."

She stiffened. "Who are you?"

"I'm not dangerous, please let me speak to you."

Charlotte's purchases were already past the cash desk. Félix stared at them rather than at the journalist who was trying to get away. He paid for his aftershave as she closed her bags. She looked at him. "Who are you?" she asked again. He explained what his job was, told her about the investigation and what had brought him here; he showed her his pass for the law court, and she relaxed a little and agreed to have a quick cup of coffee with him, just next door.

There, leaning over the table so he wouldn't have to talk too loud, she listened to him recounting the details of the Nice affair, how Louchsky's name kept reappearing and how he had stumbled on Lira's articles on the Internet. In return she told him about how she had met Lira long ago in St Petersburg during an earlier investigation, and how she had been to see her in hospital when she had heard about the attack.

"And you haven't had any more news of her?"

"No," she lied. "Just a demand for a right of reply from Louchsky's lawyer, who thought my piece was full of libellous insinuations…"

"Rassmussen."

"Do you know him?"

"Not really, just another client on the Côte d'Azure."

There were some awkward silences, and a certain solemnity, hardly broken by the sound of glasses and cups clinking behind the counter. Charlotte kept touching the lobes of her ears as though she had lost her earrings, or was trying to avoid the issue. They were both wary, although not necessarily of one another. The embarrassment was almost tangible – the stakes were so high, after all.

"Isn't there anyone, a friend perhaps, who could introduce me to her?" Félix asked.

Charlotte MacKennedy shook her head. She didn't give him Nwankwo's name. And Félix didn't tell her what he had. Conversation soon ran out. Finally she asked him for his details, just in case. Félix pulled out a notebook, tore out a page, and wrote down his number, asking her to get in touch if she heard anything. She did the same, pulling a fat diary out of the chaos of her handbag and handing him a card, held between red-varnished fingertips. They separated on the pavement. He watched her as she walked back towards the office, turning round occasionally to make sure he wasn't following her. Her shopping bag swung on her arm. It was certainly heavy…

Suddenly Félix realized that the shampoo he had seen sliding by on the mat was for blondes, and Charlotte MacKennedy was a brunette! That was why the pants she had bought had been out of character. She wasn't shopping for herself, it must be stuff for Lira. All he needed to do was wait for her to come back out of the office and then follow her. The journalist would lead him to Lira.

Two hours later Charlotte MacKennedy reappeared on the pavement. Félix had had nothing to do but simply wait all that time, brooding and puzzling, thinking about the shampoo for blondes on the mat. He realized now that he couldn't go back to the law courts and become clerk to another judge. It was impossible, he had slipped his moorings. Charlotte crossed the road and walked a little way down. Nwankwo was waiting there in his car. He took the bag. Félix watched them from the corner of the street. They were talking through the window, which meant he was about to drive off at any minute. He would lose sight of him when he could quite clearly lead him straight to Lira. It was now or never. He would tell Nwankwo what he had with him.

He walked quickly along the pavement opposite the car, planning to cross in front of it to stop it from setting off. Charlotte only spotted him at the last minute. She opened her eyes wide, and Nwankwo turned around, alarmed. Félix put his hand in his pocket, to take out a card, or the memory stick, to show that he must be heard. What he had not foreseen was Nwankwo's police guards who, seeing him digging into his jacket, thought he had a gun and leapt on him, forcing him to the ground.

Charlotte shouted: "Don't hurt him, that's the man I was just telling you about." Nwankwo got out, and told the policemen to release him. He helped Félix up, checked that he wasn't armed and suggested that he get into the car. Charlotte hesitated, but Nwankwo told her to go back to her office. "The less you know the better." He set off, but only drove a few yards and parked the car a bit farther down the street. He was already regretting the presence of his police escort, who were protecting him, but also watching him.

Félix told Nwankwo everything: where he had come from, what he knew and above all about the documents in his possession. He spoke factually and precisely like the clerk that he was, but sometimes his voice broke and he seemed to be begging: let me get close to you, come with you for the next few days, join my powerlessness to yours; let me help you, we've both lost a lot, let's put what we have left together. He felt no reciprocal warmth from Nwankwo, who stared at him fixedly, trying to gauge what sort of person he was.

"If what you say is true, you're mad to wander around London alone."

"You know where she is."

This, from Félix, was a statement, not a question.

"Lira is blind, she can't help you."

"You have no idea what's in here – thousands of names, transactions, it's dynamite!"

"Have you got a mobile?" Nwankwo finally asked. "Turn it off and remove the battery. I'll take you there. Lira will be happy to know that there's someone who needs her."

Lira was in the garden, barefoot on the grass, her legs slightly apart, her arms hanging loose, her fists closed tight. She slowly advanced one foot and then the other, then raised her fist, advanced again and punched. She willed her body to remember the moves; she recited a kata, one of the very first sequences she had learnt. She looked like someone walking on a tightrope, or in their sleep. It was slow and soft compared with what she had been able to do in the past, but she understood more clearly than ever what these gestures in the void really meant: imaginary combat was all she had left, an imaginary combat with herself, with invisible enemies in front, behind, to the side. She had to keep turning, taking her bearings in the space around her. She repeated the same gesture five, ten times over, each time a little faster. The policeman from Scotland Yard, instructed by Nwankwo to stay there, watched in amazement.

Eventually Lira paused, her body unsteady. She asked the policeman:

"Tell me, is the house on that side?"

"Yes."

She smiled. She still knew where she was. She could feel the house near her, not just as a shadow but as a solid mass. She walked straight forwards, her hands before her, balancing with her arms. When she reached the door, she sat gently down on the porch steps. With her eyes hidden behind her huge dark glasses she could have been just an ordinary woman catching the last rays of the sun.

She didn't know anything about this house that Nwankwo had brought her to, just that it was normally lived in by a family with children. On the first evening he had run her a bath. He had put two chairs next to the bathtub, a towel

175

on one, the other for her to sit on. He had led her there, helped her sit down, taken off her shoes, and folded the jumper she handed to him. Then he had gone out, promising to stay just the other side of the door in case she needed help. She had undressed and groped her way into the hot water, holding on tight to the edge of the bathtub. On the bottom she could feel one of those rubber mats put there to stop small children from slipping. He had left it there for her. She must have stayed too long in the water: when she tried to get out the heat of the bath combined with the darkness and steam around her had made her dizzy and she lost her balance. She had called out and he had come back in. She was naked and dripping, crouched prudishly against the bathtub, laughing so as not to cry. He had picked up the towel and wrapped it round her, had helped her to get up and sit down.

"Sorry to inflict the sight of a cripple on you," she had muttered.

"That wasn't what I saw," he had replied.

She was now trying to make herself familiar with this refuge. She imagined it having flowery lampshades, armchairs with high armrests, glass-fronted walnut cupboards – what she saw as a typical English interior, or any typical interior. She had never been interested in decor, always thinking that there would be plenty of time for that when she was old and unable to do much outside. Now it was too late. Back at home in St Petersburg there were photographs that would never be framed, naked light bulbs, curtains that wouldn't be changed, walls with yellowing paintwork... She went back there in her mind, guided by memory and regrets. She wandered like a ghost through her rather chaotic flat, along the bookcases with photos of Polina along their edges. September 1989, the year she was born – a beautiful baby in a pink cardigan with red flowers knitted by her mother. Next to that, the following year, Polina was sitting on a wooden horse on an old-fashioned carousel, held by

Dmitry's invisible hands. Lira went from one photograph to the next, from one year to the next. She wanted to hold on to them all, trying to remember the date, the place, the colour of the sky, the clothes in each one; she worked on her memory as though it was a muscle, she was determined not to forget. Her memories would be her eyes.

She could clearly see the photo of herself at thirteen, en pointe, a perfect little girl in a tutu, her hair in a gleaming chignon, her large blue eyes raised to the ceiling. She had just won the first prize at the Conservatoire. That photo had been at her parents' house for a long time, until they replaced it with the one of her wedding to Dmitry. They only liked pictures of their daughter in fancy dress.

Dmitry must have called them. Her father would be sighing, complaining that she had never done the right thing. Her mother, as usual, would be secretly crying and supporting her. Lira banished these thoughts from her mind. Another photo: last winter, she was laughing on a windy seashore by the Baltic. The person who took it must have loved her to make her look so beautiful, and yet the affair hadn't lasted long.

Beyond the bookcase was the leather armchair and the big mirror with the chipped gilt frame. Lira might have been a busy woman who didn't bother with much make-up, but she would glance at herself in it morning and evening, moving her head, adjusting her hair, moistening her lips, doing everything to like what she saw. All that was over. She had lost sight of herself now.

She was learning now to plunge down into her memories as others plunge into sleep. She blocked sadness off, biting back the rising tears, tried to avoid brooding on the question that tormented her: would it have been better if she had died? The simplest solution would be just to collapse, everybody would understand. But crying was forbidden. She would remain upright before all these mirrors that now served no purpose.

A car stopped. Two doors slammed, there were two people walking across the gravel. Lira stiffened.

"It's me, Lira!" Nwankwo shouted, guessing how frightened she would be. "I've brought the string you wanted. And we've got a visitor."

Lira got up slowly, her hand on the wall of the house. She didn't very much like the smell of this visitor, but she liked his first words.

"I've been looking for you," Félix said.

New Scotland Yard.
Report From Detective Inspector Dave Smith.
15th September

Nwankwo Ganbo has installed the blind Russian journalist Lira Kazan in his house at 22 Dawson Street, Oxford.

She does not often leave the house, occasionally spends some time in the garden.

Ganbo stays with her.

For the last two days another man has joined them in the morning. His first name is Félix. He is French. Photo attached.

They shut themselves in the sitting room. They seem to be working.

Microphones have been installed.

And then there were the nights. "Lie down, Lira. Relax, breathe. It's going to be all right. I'm here…" Nwankwo spoke to her like that each time the nightmares started again. She called, he came running. He would find her sitting up, sobbing. There was no point turning the light on. Nwankwo would sit beside her, holding her hand, in the big room with the double bed where he used to sleep with Ezima.

At first they had been awkward together, linked only by their rigid determination to continue, but that stage had now passed. He was no longer the hyper-tense and over-polite teacher, who seemed to deny the folklore and loud laughter of his own people. And she was no longer the kind of woman who couldn't stand the emotions and tears of other women.

And so they did the best they could, clinging to one another. Nwankwo was caught between two worlds, two lives; Lira between her memories and the total darkness that surrounded her.

The empty house was now laced with pieces of string stretched between the rooms, a curious idea that Lira had borrowed from the old blind man in St Petersburg. During the day she would guide herself around by feeling the string with the tips of her fingers; at night he would run his finger along it – in his other, normal life he would have been stumbling over his children's toys. Now he was woken up, not just by Lira's nightmares, but by his own. At the faintest sound of an engine outside, or the smallest flicker of head-lights he would be up and standing against the window of his room, which he had chosen because it was at the front of the house. Two targets in the same house – it was just too dangerous. The protection supplied by the British police would soon be withdrawn. Nwankwo was not sorry – he had broken his promise, and the police must know that.

They would have to leave.

Lira often heard him pacing up and down. She thought about something Dmitry had often accused her of: he said that all this activity of hers was simply a way of escaping from intimacy and a private life, of freeing herself from the fear of actually having to confront real life. During the silences of her imaginary conversations with him she wanted to retort that where she was hiding now fear was a permanent condition, with hostile armies lurking among the shadows. But of course, deep down she knew that he was right. It wasn't Louchsky's plots that were making her cry out in the night, it was just her terrible loneliness.

And then there were the days. Each morning, in the privacy of her bedroom, Lira would rehearse a few movements, gestures of avoidance and defence which demanded total precision from her hips, ankles and hands. She had already broken a lamp with her karate moves but it didn't matter; she gained a sense of continuity from the pursuit of these old exercises and challenges. She liked to believe that the half, quarter and full turns that she practised between these four walls would help her to walk straight ahead when the time came to set off alone along a street. But when would that be?

Félix arrived around eleven each morning, after an hour's drive. The room was filled with his over-strong scent. "Well like that I always know you're there," Lira had said. She had let her hands wander over his shoulders, his face, his hair – "You know, I've never seen you". They quickly got to work. Everything they had already known about the vast secret system, the international connections and complicit banks, but had been unable to prove – it was all there now in black and white. But there was an enormous amount of material and it all had to be deciphered. Félix sat in front of the computer on the dining-room table and read out the deposits, the withdrawals and, line by line, dates, names and figures. He spoke entirely in abbreviations. Lira sat curled up on the sofa, listening and repeating them to herself in whispers as though trying to imprint information that she could not read onto her brain. Nwankwo, for his part, took notes and drew arrows and diagrams. Of the three, he was the teacher: he had certainly trawled through plenty of bank statements during his career as an investigator.

"Forex means cash withdrawals," he said.

They had quickly identified Finley's accounts, and Louchsky's as well. With one simple addition of four transfers from Lichtenstein into Finley's account, Nwankwo was able to conclude with a sigh: "It's like a subscription – eighty million dollars a year!"

"Meaning?" Lira asked.

"The petrol company drilling in the desert pays Finley a few centimes per litre and credits it to the Lichtenstein account."

Sometimes his voice would fade away, as though crushed by all that money, and he would appear to be absent for a few seconds as his thoughts wandered back to his homeland; then he would once again pick up his pencil and get back to work on his arrows and bank accounts. A lot of the payments went directly to their recipient, revealing the sense of impunity that reigned at the top of the pyramid. Others went through under the cover of code names and offshore companies that Nwankwo noted down in order to check later on the Internet. Sometimes it was enough to look up old newspaper articles or accounts of past business transactions, and cross-check them with the bank statements to find out who had been involved in Louchsky or Finley's business dealings.

As the day went by, the low table became covered in mugs, plates, crumbs, pieces of ham or cake left over from improvised meals. Nwankwo and Félix watched Lira, looking out for signs of fatigue showing through the dark glasses she wore to hide her lifeless eyes that were still circled with raw skin. She proudly insisted that she was fine, often mocking her own clumsiness and incapacity – "The poor blind girl would love a little more coffee," she would say, as if by saying it about herself she could forestall them from thinking or saying it.

On the third day she became obsessed by a new name, a company called Hilar, which had received four large sums from Louchsky. There was nothing by that name on the Internet. Lira wondered out loud what was hidden behind the name. She had worked so hard in the last few years that she knew all the links and connections within the Louchsky empire. Looking at her you might have the impression that blind people either become possessed by their illusions or lose them entirely. She longed to be indispensable, impossible to fault, as nimble as Félix's fingers on the keyboard or Nwankwo's pencil on his notebook.

"Well, apart from the Minister of Defence's dog, I've never heard that name…" Félix sighed finally.

"A dog, did you say?" Nwankwo asked.

"Yes it's some kind of Labrador, he was always posing with it in *Nice-Matin*, that's our local paper. But I'm talking about when he was regional president."

"What sort of guy is he, your minister?"

"Arrogant, ambitious, part of the Élysée inner circle. He's often talked about as the possible next prime minister."

"It might be a possible track to follow…"

"What, because of his dog?"

"Sometimes the only things powerful men still love are their animals, you know…" Lira said.

A dog providing a powerful man with a hunter's image. A dog leading a blind woman. A lot of images sprang to Lira's mind, and she suppressed them as well as she could. The advantage of all these figures was that they in some way protected her by removing her from the normal world in which she no longer had a place, apart from that reserved for the disabled, exposed to the pitying stares of other people. The figures formed a dark circle around her; they were concealed, invisible to the rest of the world – only she, Lira, could see them. They seemed to produce sparks in her brain, and then she felt like David facing Goliath. At these moments she was bathed in a soft euphoria, but never for long: each point gained increased the risk they were taking, and then a kind of sticky fear would inhabit their minds and bodies – not just Lira's but Nwankwo's and Félix's too. Fear affected them all and came between them.

Félix left at around six. The evenings were long after that. At first Nwankwo hadn't dared turn on the television, for fear of seeming to taunt Lira, but then it was she who asked him to. After that the glowing screen made this strange, upside-down household sound much the same as all the others at that time of night. They would watch the news and talk about it. Lira, not being a child of the Commonwealth, did not understand everything, and Nwankwo would explain. Then he would often give her the remote, putting her thumb on the buttons so that she could clumsily surf the channels. She would usually stop on a music channel – the throbbing rhythms of rock music had always made her feel good.

In the evenings too she would dictate letters to Nwankwo to send to her daughter. They were in English, not even in their own language, and filled with lies – she said she was fine, and that they would meet soon. Lira ended by covering the letters with kisses and words they had used since Polina's babyhood. She missed her and yet she dreaded seeing her; it was as though her daughter's gaze would confirm once and for all the permanence of her blindness. Then Nwankwo would write the address on the envelope: "Poste restante. Nîmes. France." Outside the nights were beginning to draw in. It was getting colder too. And there was no more police protection; only an emergency number in the kitchen, just in case.

US EMBASSY, COPENHAGEN

CONFIDENTIAL

SECTION 01.081685

SEPTEMBER 17

SUBJECT: MEETING BETWEEN AMBASSADOR AND SUNLEIF
STEPHENSEN

BANKRUPT FAROESE BANKER SUNLEIF STEPHENSEN HAS AC-
CEPTED THE PROTECTION PROGRAMME OFFERED BY THE CIA.
HE WILL BE EVACUATED TO THE UNITED STATES.

"You were more fun when you were a civil servant."

That's what Mark had said the previous night. Félix had not replied, because it was true. His insomnia left him more and more often at the edge of the bed, exhausted but unable to sleep, tossing and turning between the sheets, while Mark lay next to him breathing deeply in a mildly alcoholic doze. He could have moved closer to him and woken him up, but he didn't have the strength, or even the will, to do it. A part of him always remained in the Oxford house with the other two. He knew nothing of Lira's nightmares and Nwankwo's nocturnal roaming, but he could guess at them.

The telephone rang. He had gone to sleep late and it seemed to come from far away. It continued to ring insistently. Since nobody was answering it and the cat had climbed onto the bed, and since it was ten o'clock and Mark had gone, Félix finally got up and grabbed the receiver. He heard a familiar voice against the background of a strange noise, almost like a hairdryer. It was the judge, sitting behind the counter at Max's – the barber who had been cutting his hair for the last fifteen years in his shop at the top of Rue Gioffredo in Nice. He had been reduced to using his barber's telephone. The barber didn't ask questions and even imagined some kind of sinister affair that might give his shop the air of a hideout, with its plastic seats and tired sign outside. Félix was suddenly wide awake.

The judge was speaking very fast; sometimes there was the sound of a bell in the background, either from the door or the till, where Max was busy charging thirty-five euros for a cut and blow-dry to a heavily backcombed lady. Anyway the news was good: the judge had found a mention of a company called Hilar in the penal records, the computer archive of all victims and perpetrators of crimes and misdemeanours. There had been a complaint three years ago about neighbourhood troubles from the director of the company, a lady living in a two-bedroom apartment in Nice.

"Félix, you'll never guess who came in to make the complaint! It was Douchet's wife!"

"Douchet's wife…" Félix repeated, under his dishevelled hair. "She was on the yacht for Linda Stephensen's little party that night."

He took a shower in record time, got dressed and rushed to Oxford. He was late but wildly excited.

"It's a bombshell, my friends. Douchet is the minister with the dog! Hilar is a company run by his wife! Louchsky was paying bribes to one or other of them!"

He told them at high speed about the judge's call, the hairdresser, the archives. Nwankwo and Lira listened dumbstruck. Each one was thinking about their own piece of the story, their particular enemy, their part of the world. But things were coming together and they were jubilant. They had struck gold with proof that a French minister was taking money from Louchsky. Then Lira began to enumerate all the hundreds of scams she knew about, repeating lists of figures in a monotonous voice, reeling off an inventory of Louchsky's villainy.

"We'll expose it all, we must call the press," she said.

"It's just what Charlotte MacKennedy has been waiting for!" Félix added.

"Not now!" Nwankwo snapped.

He sometimes spoke sharply in a tone that was not to be contradicted. In other times, Lira would have flown at him. But she kept quiet – she respected him, and she depended on him. Félix also bit back his words. They set to work again, now seeing everything in the light of this new information, their minds churning. They settled down, returned to the figures and put their differences aside.

After a couple of hours, Lira said: "I need to go out, I want to walk, I want to hear some noise." It was as though the news had given her wings.

The other two sprang to attention and a trip into town was hastily arranged. It was the middle of the afternoon, the weather was warm, and there were crowds on the pavements. Nwankwo played the role of bodyguard, looking around constantly, walking first in front and then behind the other two. Oxford, with its churches, colleges, libraries and cafés, and all the old stained-glass windows and ancient oak floors, seemed to be studded with potential traps. Félix gazed around him at the ancient buildings and the Gothic spires ringing out the time. Seeing the privileged students with their devouring ambition awakened his youthful revolutionary instincts. He did not wish to admire the splendour of the city – all he saw was the tyranny of convention in this cradle of an elite which would soon become as docile and silent as its predecessors. He liked to think that he was in charge of his own life, and that nobody else would ever make any decisions for him. He felt that having Lira on his arm was one of the finest things he had ever been called upon to do.

"Are you all right?" he asked her.

"It's strange, it's like going into a dark room and feeling that you are being stared at from all sides, but much, much more intense than that…"

She had been to Oxford before and her brain was processing the images she remembered. But now she felt everything as an invisible mass. She knew that the buildings were high because she could sense them like a huge weight above her head; she felt the passers-by going past by the movement of air on her face; she guessed that the door of a shop or restaurant was opening by the sudden gust of warm air against her body. She had become sensitive to every minute change in the atmosphere and could even tell whether she was in a street or a cul-de-sac. But it was all so intense and fast-moving that after half an hour she had had enough. It was all too much for her, the noise, the movement, all those shapes above and around her. This sudden return to the real world reminded her cruelly of everything she had lost, and of how concentrated she would have to remain in order to survive. They went back to the car. Lira said nothing. She had thought that this outing would do her good, but now she felt that it had just been a waste of time.

They drew up in front of the house. Before Nwankwo had even switched off the engine he noticed a shape in the window. He silently pointed it out to Félix.

"What's going on?" Lira immediately asked.

"It looks as though someone has taken advantage of our expedition to pay us a visit," Félix replied.

"It shows they know perfectly well where we are," said Nwankwo.

"Who's 'they'?"

"There are plenty of 'them' to choose from!"

"What shall we do? Shall we go in?"

"No. We could be shot down like rabbits. And we've got all the important stuff with us."

He didn't care about his possessions, his memories – all that mattered were the computer and the notebooks on the back seat. Nwankwo put the car into reverse, turned around and they set off. For a while nobody dared ask where they were heading. Nwankwo didn't know either. He kept his foot flat on the accelerator, his eyes on the mirror, and instinctively headed towards London.

"We'll go to Mark's flat." Félix finally broke the silence. "After that we'll see."

They left the house far behind them. Inside, drawers and cupboards had been opened, beds turned upside-down. Two men stood paralysed on the landing. They had thought they still had plenty of time. They had knocked everything over. Their orders were not to kill, just to make it look like an ordinary burglary, and to get hold of the computer on which "the blind girl, the African and the little gay frog", as Scotland Yard called them, had been working. Three *sputniks*, Lira would have called them.

The Guardian, 22nd September

There have been mixed reactions from NATO countries to the signature on Monday of an agreement to create a joint venture between Russian naval construction company KUT, controlled by oligarch Sergei Louchsky, and the French company DVTS for the construction in France of two Mistral-class warships for the Russian navy, with further plans for the building of nuclear submarines. The Baltic countries and the United States view this agreement with the greatest suspicion as it is a first for any nation within the Atlantic alliance.

The agreement has been signed within a few days of the expiry date for tenders put out by Russia for the construction of a multi-purpose cruiser capable of transporting helicopters and tanks. Discussions have been taking place for several months, stalling mainly on the question of shared technology. The two parties have agreed on "concrete elements" for cooperation, but have chosen not to announce them for the moment. This is clearly the part of the deal that is of particular interest to the other NATO countries. The order is worth €1.27bn, according to a source close to the interested parties.

The new consortium would then be in a position to bid for other tenders for the construction of "a fourth generation of civil and military ships, and submarines" according to a statement with no further details from the chairman of DVTS, quoted by Russian news agencies.

"Now's the moment!" Félix said.

"No," Nwankwo kept repeating.

But this time Félix wouldn't back down. He waved the *Guardian* in front of him. The paper had just supplied them with the clearest reason for the commissions paid by Louchsky to Douchet – a huge military construction deal. He repeated what Steffy had told him over the telephone about the large contract that was preoccupying the Quai d'Orsay – and here it was all over the papers! In France the announcement was being treated as a great coup. Dockyards that had been partially laid off for the past four months were now celebrating the fact that they would be back at full strength.

"The key word," said Lira, "is shared technology. That's what Louchsky is paying for."

"And that's what they're hardly mentioning. It's up to us!" Félix continued.

But they had no levers, no newspaper in which to write, no official status, no procedure they could follow. Lira's magazine in St Petersburg had been ransacked one night shortly after the attack on her. All the computer records had been destroyed, and the damage had been such that publication of the magazine was now temporarily suspended. Helen still remained deaf to Nwankwo's pleas. He had tried over and over again, with no success. As for the judge, he had been transferred and was now dealing with the statistics of juvenile delinquency.

"We must ring Charlotte," Lira said, backing Félix up.

"No," Nwankwo repeated. "We still haven't got enough ammunition – they can easily shut us up and hush up the whole affair. We've only got one chance, one shot, and now is not the moment."

"So when is the moment? What are we going to do? Look how we're living! Look around you! Look at our stupid faces! Don't you think we need help? Something's got to happen. You can't make all the decisions on your own, Nwankwo. We've reached a dead end, we're caught in a trap, we're sitting on dynamite, it's going to blow up in our faces, we've got to get out of this—"

"Shut up!" Lira shouted.

Nwankwo grabbed his jacket and left, slamming the door. They didn't know where he was going, perhaps to see his children at the other end of town. Would he knock on the door or would he just wait at the end of the street in the hope of catching a glimpse of them? He never talked about them. He had built an impenetrable wall between the two halves of his life. Each day he had become harder, more methodical, intent only on the work in front of them. Félix found his abruptness hard to take; only Lira had seen the gentleness and attentiveness he was capable of.

"Don't be angry with him," she said.

"I can't stand him."

Lira sat for a long time, silent on the unfolded grey-velvet sofa bed, absorbing his words. They had been held together by their convictions and by their setbacks, and now these were coming between them. The friendship between the three of them was being gnawed at by fear, exhaustion and impatience, and yet it was the only thing that could save them.

"Before he went to Paris, Mark said he would prefer it if you were gone before he got back. That'll be in two days' time," Félix said.

"All right, let's call Charlotte, we can go and see her and see how the land lies," Lira said softly. "But we're not doing anything without Nwankwo," she warned him.

Nwankwo, heading towards his family, could already hear Ezima's reproaches – he hadn't been to see them for two weeks. The welcome was just as he had predicted. The little one stayed back, clasping her mother's legs, Baïna jumped up to his neck: she had put on pink nail varnish and was acting like a protective little wife. Tadjou, the eldest, remained quiet, but tried to catch his father's eye, as if to gain his approval. Ezima spoke for him. She said he was unhappy in England, and so he was going home; he was flying out the next day and would live with his uncle in Lagos and go back to school there. She would soon join him there with the girls. She spoke quietly, while her cousin looked on, furious and reproachful, her arms folded. Nwankwo would have liked to have been consulted, but he knew that it would be useless to say anything. Ezima would just reply that he had done enough damage, and she would be right.

He went over to his son and put his arm around his shoulder. He pulled him over to a corner where they could be alone.

"So you're going home?"

"Yes, Pa."

"You're going tomorrow… You're lucky. I miss our country, you know. I hope I'll go back too one day and then we can all be together again."

The teenager did not reply.

"Will you go and see your grandfather? See how he is, eh?"

"Yes," Tadjou nodded. "And you, how are you?" he asked.

He suddenly seemed so grown-up all of a sudden, this son who had now reversed things and was the one worrying about his parents. And he looked so like Nwankwo! Ever since he was born, people had been saying that this boy was a replica of his father – and now it was time for him to fly away, and to think of his own future. Nwankwo looked around at the cousin's over-decorated and brightly coloured house, full of knick-knacks: it was right that Tadjou should escape from these surroundings. And then Nwankwo had a wild idea. It was as though the boy was suddenly just an extension of himself. He groped inside his pocket, pulled out a memory stick and placed it in Tadjou's hand, which was as long and slender as his own. He whispered: "Put this in the bottom of your suitcase, give it to your uncle and tell him to go and see Kay at the port, he'll understand…"

Tadjou's eyes shone. At last his father was taking some notice of him. Nwankwo gave him a manly hug. They were both stiff, the father like a solid block, obsessed with one thing only, the son resisting any childish gestures now that he was being treated like an adult. From now on, he too would be in danger.

Before he left, Nwankwo wrote a cheque to the cousin, who was still looking daggers at him. He embraced each of his children. Ezima let him carry on. She understood from the tension in the air and the size of the cheque that he wouldn't be back for a long time.

He hadn't gone more than ten steps down the street when he felt a rising nausea, with painful cramps in his stomach and a terrible sense of exhaustion. He walked on a little and then leant against a wall, vomiting up his guts and his whole life.

The sound of Charlotte's stiletto heels clicking along the floor towards her reminded Lira what it was like to be a beautiful woman; those clicking heels that said "I am powerful and I am attractive" – it was a performance she would never again take part in. And then she found herself enveloped by Charlotte's arms and by her voice, a little too solicitous for her liking. She settled down with them, ordered some tea, and Félix gave the broad outlines of the situation. They had agreed beforehand what they would and would not say and all they gave her were a few Grind Bank statements in which Louchsky's name appeared as well as an account of Eyvin's death.

"We just need to know what you think to start with, that's all. Nwankwo isn't keen and we won't do anything without him."

Of course Charlotte was excited – "It's a big story," she said – and she needed to speak to her editor as soon as possible. Félix was excited too, what he had always dreamt of was about to take place: a victory over secrecy. Both their voices sounded like water about to boil over. Lira shivered listening to them – she could hear herself, she had been just the same, pushing open Igor's door demanding extra space in the magazine. But today she just repeated that they must still convince Nwankwo before doing anything.

The next day, as they had agreed, Félix went down to the telephone box to ring Charlotte. Even Mark's landline might not be safe. As he went into the handsome red box that had been the cover illustration on his English textbook at school, he reflected that nowadays they were only used by poor people and tramps. Charlotte suggested a meeting with the editor in two hours' time, and she gave the address of a suitable café. Félix agreed. When he told Lira she hesitated, torn between the need to act quickly and an unthinkable quarrel with Nwankwo. She said to Félix that she would try and get hold of him while Félix was out, and that he must on no account give them anything concrete.

Félix changed trains more often than was necessary to ensure that he wasn't being followed. When Nwankwo reappeared Lira told him about the meeting with the editor of the *Guardian*. Nwankwo punched the wall in a fury.

Félix turned off his mobile and took the battery out five stations before he reached his destination. "We had to do it," Lira murmured to Nwankwo, telling him about the first meeting. Nwankwo didn't speak. He just clenched his jaw. He couldn't bring himself to be angry with Lira.

Félix pushed open the door of a café, well off the beaten track, away from any possible dangerous encounter. He wanted to see the truth about Eyvin's fate, his anonymous death, in enormous headlines. He wanted to avenge all the humiliations he had suffered, all those mornings spent reading about unpunished crimes in the Nice newspapers. Nwankwo and Lira remained immobile, facing one another, almost without breathing, enveloped by the crushing silence of the apartment. Lira could hear all the distant sounds of the building: doors squeaking, telephones ringing, taps running.

Félix gave Charlotte and the editor Eyvin's name, as well as his position at Grind Bank, the date of his arrival in Nice, his flight, his disappearance and presumed time of death a few miles outside London. "We haven't given them anything yet, and we won't without you," Lira promised Nwankwo.

"But you have done it, haven't you?" he retorted.

Félix showed them a few extracts from the documents that Eyvin had been carrying, a few names too, and a few accounts, including Louchsky's, all hinting at the magnitude of the sums involved as well as of the dangers he was incurring. He gave them nothing to take away, but they took notes. When he got back, Nwankwo pointed a threatening finger at him.

"You can tell yourself one thing: on the morning, or even the night before the story appears in the paper it won't be just one or two assassins on our tracks. At least we'll be dead when the story gets suppressed, we won't have to see that!"

"Fuck it Nwankwo! Stop treating me like a naive student. I was the one who went to pick up the CDs. You might at least let me have some say in what we do with them!"

Nwankwo didn't listen. He went out, ignoring Lira's shouts: "Next time don't bother to come back, either of you! The blind girl can look after herself!" She listened to his steps disappearing down the passage, the lift doors opening. They could go in and out as much as they liked. She wouldn't be slamming any more doors.

Nwankwo walked aimlessly, something he never normally did. This sort of area was unfamiliar to him, with its warm lights in the dusk, its restaurants and pubs full of well-dressed white men and women. Nwankwo felt alienated from these places where people were having fun, trying to make their lives a little less dreary. Why did doors always slam wherever he was staying? What would Uche do on a night like this? He would probably go into a pub, order a beer, then another and another, laughing in anticipation of approaching drunkenness. He said orphans had no choice but to invent stories. Nwankwo couldn't do that. He had lived for so long with danger at his back: he could hear the voices of his father and grandfather warning him: "The toad doesn't come out in the afternoon without a reason." You couldn't unlearn fear. Nwankwo went into a pub as though Uche was holding the door open for him; he ordered a beer, and then another – he loved that first moment with the brimming glass and the froth on his lips. He looked around at the other people lined up at the bar, with their elbows at the same angle as his. It was nice to be like other people for once, and it was so rare. He thought of Félix and Lira, still up in the flat, particularly of Lira who from now on would be inhabiting another world. What went on inside the mind of a blind person? Or anyone's mind, for that matter? He had no idea. And he had no idea where they were all heading.

High Court of Justice
Queen's Bench Division
Action HQ09

Plaintiff JMD
Versus
1) Guardian News and Media Limited
2) Persons unknown

The defendant may not make use of, publish, communicate or reveal to any other party any information or document mentioning the plaintiff until 10th December. The defendant must retain any such documents for the use of the plaintiff or his representative in case they are needed for defence purposes.

If the defendant does not obey this injunction he may be called to appear in court, its directors may serve a prison sentence or face a fine or confiscation of property.

Charlotte was dumbstruck. How could they have known? All she had done was copy out a few of the main points and the general trend of the statements shown to her by Félix. She had not signed the piece so that there could be no link with Lira, and somebody else had rung the police for details about Eyvin's death. But that had been enough to unleash the diabolical machinery of power. There was no way of knowing where the first telephone call had come from, but you could be sure it was from the very top. In the land of the tabloid there is a means of preventing journalists from telling the truth about such things as money laundering, known as a super-injunction. It is usually applied at the very last moment. This one had come to the *Guardian* at six o'clock: publication forbidden. The procedure had been set in motion by Jonas Rassmussen. The name of his client was withheld, replaced by random initials. This was allowed by the law since it existed to preserve a person's good name.

For the editor this wasn't the first time – he had suffered injunctions before and he went into crisis mode. You had to obey an injunction, but he promised to fight it and launch an appeal. But of course it was too late, and soon the other side would force the paper to reveal its documents and its sources.

Those sources, once again, became the quarry, pursued by hounds.

When the telephone rang at Mark's flat, Félix was standing with his back to the room facing the window. He wasn't saying anything; Nwankwo too had become completely silent. Félix was watching the street. There was a car down below with two men inside. One had got out, goodness knows where he was now, perhaps in the lift on his way up, or in the corridor listening... Who was he? One of Finley's heavies trying to finish Nwankwo off? Or a Russian going after Lira again? Nwankwo had a third candidate: the British secret service. He was already convinced that they had been the ones searching the Oxford house.

The phone went on ringing. Finally Félix picked up the receiver. He recognized Charlotte's voice, trembling: "Injunction," she said.

"What's an injunction?"

Nwankwo froze. He knew perfectly well what it was. Then he exploded.

"That's our death sentence! This country is a tax haven and a judicial haven too. The Prime Minister can stop any investigation he feels like, he can block any story. There are billions of pounds hidden over here, think of all the people they could save, and it's been going on like this for years, decades, a century! And you think you can overturn all that by feeding one miserable little story to the papers. I told you, it's no longer enough, you've got to think bigger than that, time's running out. Thanks to your stupidity they'll be emptying out the accounts as we speak and giving assassins their orders to kill us!"

Lira was shaking. "I'm going to call the embassy. It's over, I'll go home. Dmitry was right. You carry on with all that stuff you've got, it's huge. I'm just slowing you down. I can't contribute anything. I've told you everything I know."

"Don't talk rubbish, Lira," Nwankwo said drily.

His rage suddenly evaporated as he looked over at her face. She had taken her glasses off and you could see her eyes, her wounds and her tears. Were they because she had given up the fight, or had she just accepted her fate? Her face was pale and drawn. She had never rested as the doctors had told her to. And she hadn't been to see the shrink who would have talked her through the moment her life had been overturned. And the two men supporting her, the men who had become her eyes – they were now equally lost.

The three of them had never imagined themselves being outside the law; they had always felt that they were on the side of righteousness, inside the machinery of legality, however rusty it might have become. Now here they were, spied on, eavesdropped on, pursued by government forces, their lives threatened by mafiosi. All their pursuers, for all their different methods and orders, had one common purpose: the destruction of the documents. The inner workings of political and financial dealings must remain buried out of sight.

A key suddenly turned in the door. They all jumped. The silhouette of a small man appeared in the doorway. He had a polite smile, tracksuit bottoms, slightly awkward gestures – nothing like the kind of killer they had been dreading night and day. The man was clearly unused to his arrival creating such a sensation. He explained that he had come to clean the flat, as he did every Tuesday. He looked at Lira, stared at her face for a long moment, as though he recognized something familiar in her – the fragility of a survivor. Then he went and opened a cupboard in the kitchen and got out the dusters and the vacuum cleaner, signalling that he would start with the other rooms so as not to disturb them too much. Silence soon fell again between them, so heavy that they could even hear the sound of his duster.

"I'm going out to find a hotel for tonight," Félix suddenly said.

"It's too risky to use a telephone or credit card, even for you, Félix. If they're downstairs it means they've been following you as well, and for quite a while."

"We need a gun," Lira said.

Nwankwo cleared his throat noisily to cover their voices. The cleaner passed to and fro, tidying, hovering, cleaning, restoring the flat to its original state. Nwankwo, Lira and Félix sat perched on three cushions around the computer as though it contained explosives and they were suicide bombers waiting to go into action. The walls seemed to melt away around them as they were returned to being merely those of an upwardly mobile architect's smart apartment. They had to leave. They needed to find a way out. Not for a moment did any of them envisage approaching the police. That would have meant that the documents would disappear for ever. The cleaner came back through the sitting room on his way to scrub the bathtub. Nwankwo watched him carefully.

"We'll give him some cash and send him out to get us hotel rooms," he finally said.

"If he's dressed like that any hotel would get suspicious and ask him for papers, which he probably doesn't have," Félix said. "I know – wait!" He got up.

He ran into the bedroom, like a child trying to get back in favour after being naughty, and then reappeared with one of Mark's beautifully cut jackets. Everything happened quickly after that. They asked the cleaner whether he would do them a great service – he would be paid of course – and he listened to their proposal, both surprised and amused. He had certainly guessed that these people were out of place in this flat, which would have made a perfect double-page spread in an interior-decoration magazine. He agreed to the plan, and pulled on the jacket, which fitted perfectly. Félix added one his own scarves.

"He looks very handsome," Lira said, defying them to leave her out of the game.

Félix smiled. In order to make the cleaner feel more relaxed he asked him what he was called, where he came from and what he did before coming to England.

"My name is Adit. I was a professional letter-writer and poet in India."

There was an embarrassed silence. They didn't know quite what to say and apologized. Then Félix handed him the money, reassuring him that there would be no problem with Mark. He gave him an address near St Pancras and asked him to reserve rooms for two nights, starting that evening. The man set off. Félix watched from the window as he walked along the pavement a few minutes later. His bearing had completely changed. He was a good actor. Or else all it had taken was a designer jacket and their trust in him to restore his own confidence.

Then Félix had a sudden brainwave: they would disguise themselves, become unrecognizable. There was plenty to choose from in Mark's cupboard: velvet, leather, loud patterns, sober suits. There was even a long dress that laced up the back, left over from an unforgettable drag party. And there were plenty of wigs, too, in the bathroom drawer. Félix made the suggestion. Nwankwo groaned. But no one had a better idea, and so he let himself be led over to the wardrobe, looking more and more irritated.

"I'll always be a black man."

"Yes, but with a moustache, Adit's old cap and jacket, you won't look like an Oxford don at least."

First, they would disguise themselves. Then they would leave separately. Then they would leave the country. Félix's brain was boiling. He poured out his plans at high speed as he pulled hangers out of Mark's cupboards. He didn't realize that in opening up these wardrobes he was revealing the other side of his life; his days would now be more like his nights, clandestine and secretive. And by removing Nwankwo's suit, he too was revealing his other self, the African archetype that he had always tried to escape from. Lira, sitting on the edge of the bed, waited for something to be suggested for her, as though she no longer cared about appearances. She was no longer talking about calling the embassy. She wanted to go to France – that was where Louchsky's main operation was, and that was where her daughter was.

"And that's where he's having his birthday party! He's taken over Versailles for his fortieth!" Félix said delightedly, remembering what Steffy had told him. "When is his birthday?"

"October the ninth," said Lira. She knew everything about Louchsky by heart.

Soon they had finished trying on clothes and had settled on their chosen looks. They were all agreed – they would go to France. They would find a place far from everything, out of reach of all the radars. Félix recited the address to them, it must not be written down anywhere. They agreed to meet there in eight days' time.

My dear Félix,

I think an envelope and an old-fashioned stamp are still the safest way for us to communicate. Especially as my barber won't let me use his telephone any more – he won't even cut my hair now. He believes what he has heard, you know how fast rumours travel in Nice. They won't have reached you yet and I hope I'm the first to tell you about what is happening to me.

I started three weeks ago at the juvenile courts. After a few days I began to reproach myself for having seen it as a punishment. The young people were fascinating, some of them had already begun highly promising criminal careers, but all without exception were still open to being helped. I used to take their dossiers home at night, more than we ever used to, because their stories were still being written and for the first time I felt I might be able to achieve something.

However, a few days ago I was summoned by the president of the tribunal, who informed me that a young girl had made a complaint. She claimed that I had made advances to her during an interrogation, that I had made her sit very close to me, that I had stroked her and made certain offers in exchange for a rendezvous. She was sixteen and had been caught shoplifting in a supermarket, not for the first time, and she also had a few grams of cannabis on her. I asked to see her again, to be confronted with her. The president replied that that was impossible. They must have offered her freedom in exchange for her lies. You know how it works, Félix, it's the final stage of the game, to compromise someone. That's where I've ended up. I've been suspended and told to have therapy.

Don't get angry, it won't help. And don't reproach yourself for having insisted on searching Louchsky's premises – I wanted to do it as much as you.

But that's not what's important.

I lied to you the other day, when I disappeared and young Eyvin came into the office. The scandal machine had already gone into action then – I had just received an anonymous message threatening to tell my wife about my liaison with my piano teacher. I love that woman, she has done me an enormous amount of good and given me something I never knew existed, or was incapable of seeing. And yet that day I went to tell her that it was all over. I gave her up, I went into retreat, and sent a young man to his death. I was a coward, and to what end? Just to save appearances.

That, more than anything else, is what I wanted to tell you. I know you won't believe this story of groping and blackmail, but you may be the only one. Even my wife gives me funny looks, as though I might have done what I'm accused of. I think we've finally come up against this great empty space between us, the lack of children. I am going to defend myself because I can't allow these lies to stand unchallenged, but to tell the truth this suspension suits me quite well. I have no desire to return to the law courts. And by the way, your request for unpaid leave gave great pleasure to a great many people.

I hesitated before writing to you, as I don't want to burden you with my problems, you've got plenty of your own. But what has happened to me proves that they are prepared to do anything. So be very careful.

Jean

The tall fellow in the cap putting out the dustbins at the bottom of the building was Nwankwo, dressed in the cleaner's ill-fitting blouson. Eventually he set off down Westbourne Grove, walking fast, crossing the road frequently, making sure he wasn't being followed. There were too many smart boutiques and expensive health-food shops for the street to be truly bohemian; it was full of young people who looked like his students, but Nwankwo no longer had the costume or the job that connected him with them. He felt that the smell of rubbish was clinging to him. He noticed a fine church that had been partly converted into a boutique. The church had itself been converted, rather than converting others. Here people were beautiful, healthy, young and solvent – they were not praying about the future. He walked up to Notting Hill Gate station.

Half an hour later he saw them walking slowly towards him through the crowds. Lira had a brown wig beneath a hat, dark glasses and a man's suit. She was holding Adit's arm – he had returned from his mission, still in his Paul Smith jacket. "How do we look?" she had whispered before they set off. "Super-cool," Félix had replied. He had stayed behind, gathering up his things, taking the computer and the CDs disguised as British pop music and was going back to Paris that evening. Lira clung onto Adit's arm; he put his hand on hers as if they were old friends. They looked as though they were exchanging confidences.

"Anything ahead?" she asked.

"No, no," he murmured.

"Am I walking straight?"

"You're perfect, just stay beside me."

"Anything unusual?" she asked again.

"Nothing."

Lira's mind was buzzing. It felt as though the buildings around her were pressing down on her head and each passing car almost seemed to touch her. All these massive shapes were enlarged by her fear, and closed in as though about to suffocate and crush her. She concentrated hard, listening carefully to the sounds of the crowd, to the footsteps, trying to measure distances in her head. Nwankwo waited for them to approach, they were not far away now. He suddenly noticed a car moving slowly along the street; it looked like the one that had been waiting outside Mark's building and it appeared to be following them from a distance. He leapt forwards.

"Nwankwo?" Lira said as he got level with them.

"Yes, Lira, it's me, we've been spotted, they're following us. We'll go into the Underground, we'll have to walk fast, you must trust me."

He took Lira's arm now, and explained to the man whose clothes he was wearing that he should go, things were getting dangerous. Adit murmured his farewells and gently let go of Lira, who clutched onto Nwankwo. Neither of them turned around at the sound of squealing brakes behind them. They would never know that Adit had stepped in front of the car to slow it down. They went down into the Underground.

"Who's after us, Nwankwo?"

"I don't know."

"What do they look like?"

"Brutes."

"Brutes or cops?"

"They're pretty similar sometimes, but I'd say these are brutes."

Nwankwo looked at the signs, and hesitated. Circle Line, Central Line – it was a deep station, with escalators down to the platforms.

"Hang on to me, Lira. We're going down an escalator."

She was terrified of stairs, she had said so in the Oxford house. Each step seemed like a precipice. Nwankwo dragged her down, no time to stand still. The killer was bound to be right behind them now. He counted out loud for her: "One! Two! Three! Four!" Lira went down in step with him, each one a leap into the void. She dug her nails into Nwankwo's skin, breathing heavily. The other passengers stood aside as they came down, embarrassed by the spectacle of this strange pair.

Nwankwo suddenly heard running footsteps in the passages and then complaints from people being jostled and pushed aside. The killer was nearby. They had to go deeper. There was a second escalator below the first and, gathering Lira up, Nwankwo said, "I'm going to carry you, Lira." He swept her into his arms and threw himself down the stairs, begging the crowd to let him pass. There was a maze of corridors at the bottom and he put her down.

"Can you run, Lira? It's not too crowded – just hold my hand tight. Run!"

Blind people never run, they walk. They hold a white stick, which they wave from side to side when they're lost. But Lira ran. In her mind she could see herself running along the edge of the Neva, or along a platform to catch a train. Her brain supplied enough images to keep her legs moving.

Run, Lira, run! The little voice in her head kept saying it. Her hand was crushed in Nwankwo's. He would say "Watch out, we're turning right!" and they would turn. But the footsteps behind were growing closer – where had all the other people gone? It was as though they had deserted the station on purpose, leaving them to die. Nwankwo was going too fast, pulling Lira's arm. She fell down, he picked her up, they set off again. But soon the man was there behind them, then in front of them. He had a gun stuck into his waistband.

"He's armed," Nwankwo murmured.

The man approached, his thumb on the handle of the gun. Lira recognized his voice, then his smell.

"Is that a gun in your pocket or are you just pleased to see me?" she suddenly said, in Russian.

The sentence had come out of nowhere, Nwankwo didn't understand what she was saying. But the man did, and was not amused. He came forward – he'd teach the blind girl a lesson she'd never forget. Lira let him come, holding back Nwankwo, who wanted to intervene. The man was tall, she could sense that. He let her grab his arms, quite sure that he could easily flip her onto the ground. But Lira had another phrase in her mind now, from those happy days when all the fighting she did was at karate class on Tuesday nights with Tanya: "Girls, if you're attacked in the street you've got one advantage. No one expects anything from you. You just need one surprise blow, and then you should just run." One surprise blow – there! The man was close and Lira kicked her knee up hard. The man doubled up, Nwankwo grabbed the gun and hit the assassin on the back of the neck.

"Kill him!" Lira screamed.

She was now possessed with rage, rage for life and for death. She didn't allow Nwankwo to hesitate. She was close enough to him to grab the gun, and she fired it at the lump by her feet. "One for the blind girl," she said. "Now run!" Nwankwo shouted, seizing the gun again. The man lay bleeding and moaning on the ground, his cries echoed through the corridors. A second man was probably close behind. And the surveillance cameras were pointing down at them.

A train pulled in just as they reached the platform and they jumped in, using the crowd as cover while they discreetly removed cap, moustache and wig.

"Did I hit him?" Lira whispered.

"Yes, and you aimed well, you got him in the thigh. You didn't kill him, but he won't be moving for a while. What did you say to him?"

"Just a line from an old movie that my friend Tanya likes."

Then they were silent. Nwankwo had not let go of Lira's hand. They sat down. She was shaking, the fear was suddenly catching up on her, invading her whole body. She should have been paralysed back there in the passage, facing that man, but she hadn't allowed her terror to surface. Nwankwo didn't know what to say, except that he admired her. He looked up and down the carriage constantly, but everything appeared calm: just commuters with their own preoccupations, listening to music, reading, looking at puzzles. Each station was an ordeal, danger could reappear at any moment through the opening doors. The line on the Tube map was like a countdown for them. They were on the Central Line, they should have taken the yellow one, the Circle Line. They would have to change at Holborn onto the blue Piccadilly Line to St Pancras where their hotel was – just next to the station so that they could escape the next morning.

The hotel. Another new room to get used to, another new space to tame. The lift was too close to their room, doors kept opening and closing, a bell ringing, more possible danger. Lira lay down as soon as she came in. She was exhausted and fell into a coma-like sleep. When she woke up, Nwankwo had ordered some food. He turned on the television, to a news channel. At first nothing seemed to affect them, but all they had to do was wait. Sure enough, there was a story – a body on the Underground, shot with two bullets at Notting Hill Gate.

"Two bullets?" Nwankwo said.

"His accomplice will have wanted to shut him up. He finished him off. Louchsky will eliminate everybody, down to the last…" Lira sighed.

At the end of the news another story appeared: the death of Sunleif Stephensen, far from London, in the icy waters of the Faroe Islands. He had drowned in the sea off the shores of his home. The banker had gone out fishing alone, and the boat had been found empty. His body had been swept away into the deep waters. The newsreader implied that there might be some doubt about this so-called accidental death. There followed several interviews with British investors who had lost a great deal of money in the crash of Grind Bank. They looked as though they had drowned, in a way, as well.

"Down to the last one, I'm telling you."

Night fell. The lift brought back the last drunken night owls who reeled noisily down the corridor. And then all was quiet. The hours passed, sleepless with fear of nightmares or attack. The two of them could easily become the next two bodies on the news channels, Lira and Nwankwo, lying side by side on their twin beds.

Then Lira started to talk, a meaningless stream of words, pouring out, as though she was still running. Having finally fallen asleep she was now in the middle of a nightmare. Her arms thrashed about in the dark, she knocked over the bedside light and sat up straight in the bed. Nwankwo was already beside her, calling her, trying to wake her up and rescue her from the underground maze she seemed to be trapped in. He held her head gently against his shoulder and pushed aside the sweat-soaked hair that framed her face, his fingers lingering on her cheeks. Lira caught his hand, kissed it, pressing it against her head and her neck. *He mustn't see my eyes.*

She held the hand against her, trapping it between her head and her shoulder. Nwankwo's fingers plunged into her already tangled hair, and then slowly travelled down, willed on by both of them, onto Lira's neck, then between her breasts, and then onto her breasts. Their breathing changed pace, became heavier. Nwankwo still sat on the edge of the bed in the position of someone simply comforting her, but his hand now wandered farther, following the contours of Lira's whole body, as if to say "You're beautiful, you're complete, you were magnificent today…"

Nwankwo had never really looked at white women. They belonged, in both ways, to the opposite side of the human race; but tonight it was just the two of them, alone against the rest of the world. Lira pulled him against her, throwing her head back, letting Nwankwo's lips explore her neck. *He mustn't see my eyes.* Sometimes they stopped moving, and then started again, not quite knowing how far they would go. Eventually their fingers strayed beneath their clothes, undoing buttons and belts and their two arched bodies were completely united, from head to foot, by a surge of life and the threat of death. He came inside her – they were rescuing one another on this bed in the middle of nowhere.

222

Afterwards they lay, still entwined, their breathing becoming more regular. Soon the fear would return and they would be back in their usual places. Lira dreaded Nwankwo's first embarrassed words, the excuses he would stammer out to erase the whole event, so she spoke first:

"We're alive," she said.

US EMBASSY, COPENHAGEN

CONFIDENTIAL

SECTION 01.081720

SEPTEMBER 25

SUBJECT: SUNLEIF STEPHENSEN/WITNESS PROTECTION
PROGRAM

THE BANKER SUNLEIF STEPHENSEN HAS NOW BEEN DE-
CLARED PRESUMED DEAD BY DROWNING YESTERDAY IN THE
FAROE ISLANDS. THE STORY HAS APPEARED IN THE PRESS
AND ON TELEVISION EVERYWHERE, INCLUDING GREAT BRIT-
AIN. THE PROGRAM IS CONTINUING AS PLANNED. WHEN
STEPHENSEN ARRIVED AT THE EMBASSY HE HANDED OVER
THE GRIND BANK COMPUTER FILES. OUR SERVICES IMME-
DIATELY STARTED WORK ON THEM. STEPHENSEN APPEARED
EXTREMELY AGITATED. HE WAS BREATHING WITH DIFFICULTY
AND SPEAKING INCOHERENTLY, REPEATING OVER AND OVER
AGAIN THAT HE COULD NOT LEAVE THE ISLANDS. IT WAS
IMPOSSIBLE TO GET ANY SENSE OUT OF HIM AS HE WAS
CLEARLY IN A STATE OF SHOCK. HE KEPT ASKING THE
TIME. HE REPEATED OVER AND OVER AGAIN HIS ACCOUNT
OF HOW ALL THE EMPLOYEES HAD STREAMED OUT OF THE
BANK, OF HIS FAREWELLS TO HIS OLD GARDENER AND
ESPECIALLY TO HIS OLD NANNY WHO HAD WORKED FOR
HIM FOR TWENTY-FIVE YEARS AND WHO HAD BROUGHT
UP HIS CHILDREN. HE STARTED TO CRY. IT WAS DECIDED
THAT HE NEEDED HELP AND A TRANQUILLIZER WAS AD-
MINISTERED. HE WAS NOT SHOWN THE ACCOUNTS OF HIS
DEATH IN THE NEWSPAPERS.

TWO HOURS LATER, WE INFORMED HIM OF HIS NEW IDENTITY
AND THE ADDRESS WHERE HE WOULD BE LIVING DURING
THE NEXT FEW MONTHS. WE STRESSED HOW IMPORTANT
IT WAS THAT HIS CHILDREN SHOULD NOT BE INFORMED
FOR THE TIME BEING. HE HARDLY REACTED. HE SEEMED
MORE CONCERNED WITH THE FAROESE PRIME MINISTER'S
ANNOUNCEMENT TWO DAYS EARLIER THAT THEY WOULD BE
INSTIGATING PROCEEDINGS AGAINST HIM. HE MAINTAINED
THAT THE FAROESE GOVERNMENT WERE WELL AWARE OF THE
NATURE OF HIS ACTIVITIES AND HAD MADE NO OBJECTION
TO THEM AS LONG AS THEY WERE GOING WELL.

SUNLEIF STEPHENSEN SAID THAT JONAS RASSMUSSEN HAD
COME TO HIS HOUSE EARLY ONE MORNING ACCOMPANIED
BY ARMED MEN. THEY HAD FORCED HIM TO HAND OVER ALL
HIS PROPERTY APART FROM HIS HOUSE IN THE FAROES. THIS
RASSMUSSEN IS A LAWYER BASED IN LONDON. HE HAS ACTED
FOR SERGEI LOUCHSKY SEVERAL TIMES. THE FACT THAT HE
BECAME PERSONALLY INVOLVED WITH SUNLEIF STEPHENSEN
INDICATES THAT HE WOULD HAVE FOUND IT TOO RISKY TO
EMPLOY ANY INTERMEDIARIES. THIS IMPLIES THAT THE BANK
FILES CONTAIN IMPORTANT AND PROBABLY COMPROMISING
INFORMATION CONCERNING THE BUSINESS DEALINGS OF
SERGEI LOUCHSKY AT A TIME WHEN HE IS ABOUT TO LIST
HIS COMPANY IN THE CITY.

SUNLEIF STEPHENSEN WILL BE TRANSPORTED IN SECRET
TO THE UNITED STATES WHERE HE WILL BE GIVEN A NEW
IDENTITY.

IV

OCTOBER

"You'll see," said Dmitry... (*No, I won't see,* Lira thought) "Polina is quite safe there. It's a beautiful house with a big garden, well out of reach of any surveillance, no telephone, no television, no computers, no tax status, no bank cards or bank accounts, no electricity bill..." Dmitry was extolling the virtues of his friend. Jacques had been a film-designer; he had become allergic to modern life, with its data-gathering and surveillance cameras. Dmitry described his survival economy enthusiastically, as if it was his own. He told her about the generator, the solar panels, the wood-burning stove for cooking and heating the house, and the battery-powered radio, their only link with the outside world, on which they listened to the news each morning. Lira realized, as she listened to him talking, that after she had left him she had condemned him to a lifetime of fear. He would forever be in the position of the anxious spouse waiting for news, always dreading the telephone call that would announce her death. They had never got around to divorcing.

He had come to meet her at Gare du Nord. A friend of Félix's had told him the day and time of her arrival, ringing from a telephone box. He didn't greet Nwankwo, and just gave him a cold stare. They set off at once, driving south, towards their daughter. She didn't tell him anything about what had happened since she had left the hospital, and he didn't ask. He had put that morning behind him when the ambulance and the plane had been left waiting. But he did tell her about the political climate in Moscow, where Louchsky was growing stronger and stronger, and was now regarded as someone both influential and respectable. She could hear the challenging tone of his voice. He wanted to hear her admit that she had lost the game and that she been wrong all along, ever since they had separated.

"You're more angry with me than with him, aren't you, Dmitry?"

"One is only angry with those one used to love, Lira."

They drove for more than three hours. It was a long journey, punctuated by petrol stations and neutral remarks. The silence was disguised by the roar of the motorway. They were buried in their own thoughts. Dmitry brooded on the things he was not allowed to say, and his feeling that his life had been wasted. Lira was dreading the moment when she would have to tell her daughter that she couldn't see her, but she also dwelt on the strange and agreeable memory of her night with Nwankwo. Behind her dark glasses she almost seemed to be watching the passing landscape. When her head flopped to the side Dmitry knew that she was asleep.

Eventually the road began to wind along the edge of deep gorges, causing a sort of agitated electroencephalogram in Lira's brain. Dmitry drove slowly and carefully: he was not used to this rugged Cévennes landscape. However, the more dangerous the roads, the safer they were. The two lost Russians, Dmitry and Lira, knew nothing of the history of this mountainous area, which had held out against Julius Caesar and sheltered all manner of heretics and rebels, whose tombs are scattered along the hiking paths. Now the landscape was littered with yurts and banners denouncing the folly of the modern world. But the ancient stone walls of the houses and the streams rushing down to the villages also told their story: the sharp ridges of the Cévennes hills delineated the fortifications around a land of rebels and refugees.

"It's beautiful here, I can feel it," she said.

"Very beautiful. Breathtaking," he replied.

* * *

The car now passed an ancient wash house with a sign saying "drinking water", and crossed a narrow stone bridge. Lira knew this because she could hear the river rushing beneath her. They passed some houses – a few dogs barked as the car went by – and then pulled up a steep hill, out of the village and onto a rough and rocky road.

"What does she know?" Lira asked again.

"I've already told you… I said you had been attacked, that you were wounded, but I didn't mention your eyes. That's what you wanted isn't it?"

"Yes…"

The car stopped. "Wait for me here," Dmitry said, getting out. She heard him walking away, knocking on a door, and then quickly becoming angry and returning to the car. "Polina's not here any more." Behind him came his friend, the invisible man, explaining that it wasn't the first time she'd gone away. "She always comes back to ask if you've written, Madame. Good evening, I'm Jacques. She can't sit still here, your daughter, she senses that something isn't right and I can't very well lock her up. She's made some friends in the village, that's where she goes…"

They turned round and went back down. Dmitry was in a rage. He stopped at the bar and asked a few questions. Eventually they got an address and soon were knocking at the door.

"Get out with your stinking lies!" Polina screamed from behind the door.

"Polina, your mother is here with me, she's waiting for you in the car."

Then the floorboards creaked, the door opened and Polina flew out into the corridor without a look at her father. He watched her androgynous blonde figure disappear down the stairs. He looked into the smelly apartment and saw an open laptop. She must have Googled her mother's name and found out everything. Polina was already outside. She opened the car door and threw herself at Lira's neck, hugging her and crying "Mum". They had not seen each other for six months.

"Polina, listen, I must tell you—"

"I know, Mum."

"What do you know? No, don't take my glasses off, it's not very…"

But Polina firmly removed them. She wanted to see what had been kept from her, what had been stolen: her mother's eyes, the first eyes that had looked at her, the eyes that saw everything. There was nothing there, just two peeled, withered eyelids, glued shut. Not a hint of the light that had watched over her, that flashing shade of blue that she had inherited, not a glimmer, not a spark. A spasm of horror went through Polina's body. It was as though she too had had lost something – all her life had been contained in those eyes. Lira could sense her daughter's every convulsion. She wanted to say something, to hide, but Polina didn't give her the time. She seized her mother's face between her hands and kissed her eyes, the right hand one and then the left.

Dmitry stood on the pavement, watching them from the other side of the street. They still hugged each other in the same way as before, Polina on Lira's knee, with her legs folded and her arms around her neck. They slotted together perfectly, whatever their ages, whatever the moment, whatever Lira had done wrong. But who was comforting whom down here in the bottom of a forgotten valley in a country far from home?

Dmitry walked over, gently pushed Polina's legs down and shut the door. He got back in the car and drove the two women in his life back up to the invisible house.

"Kay!" Nwankwo shouted out loud.

A message had just appeared on the screen before him. It was the old code that he had used back there in the past:

From: k35HYT@gmail.com
To: londonsubwaystreet@gmail.com
Subject: Egbe bere

I await the signal. K.

The people around him raised their heads briefly when Nwankwo shouted, and then returned to their silent communion with their screens. For several days he had been coming back to this Parisian Internet café, charmingly called "Brave New World". He had been watching for news, for any sign from the network of coded messages that circulated among the rebels in the Delta, any indication that Tadjou had given the memory stick to the uncle, and that the uncle had handed it on to Kay. For days he had come out empty-handed, thinking that he should have known that Brave New World would be the most useless of places, and that once again everything was fucked.

And now Kay, that ace who could crack any password and cover any traces, had finally responded. He must still have been hiding in one of the containers in the port of Lagos, where he lived with a friend, two tables and three laptops linking him to the world outside. Nwankwo replied, thrilled:

From: londonsubwaystreet@gmail.com
To: k35HYT@gmail.com
Subject: Re: Egbe bere

Ugo bere
9th October
N.

He then remained seated there, his eyes gleaming behind his heavy spectacles, unable to leave this Brave New World.

Uche, you're going to see something now, this is high technology at work! You remember little Kay, we arrested him three years ago...

They had done a swoop on the back room of some business premises in Lagos; their mission had been to discover the roots of Nigerian spam as it was known, a new kind of virus that had spread through the mailboxes of millions of Western computers. It began with an appeal for help from a widow of an officer, doctor or lawyer; she needed help to withdraw a huge sum of money, promising a commission – all you needed to do as a preliminary was to supply your bank details. Of course it ended badly for anybody fool enough to respond: they had their account emptied. A lot of Americans had been suckered in this way. An African offering money – it made such a change from Africans asking for money! Of all the fraudsters arrested that day, Kay was by far the youngest and cleverest. Nwankwo and Uche had saved him from going to prison, in exchange for information, and he had become a useful ally. Now, hidden in the port, he worked on his own account and in cahoots with the opposition, and probably with the smuggling fraternity as well. He changed his container every month – he was like a cat prowling the dark corners of the docks.

Nwankwo, sitting in the Brave New World, could hear the hooting of the ships' sirens as they entered the port, the creaking of badly oiled cranes and hooks, the containers as they were unloaded, with a crash of sheet metal, and then piled up to wait, sometimes for weeks, sometimes for ever. There were fifty thousand containers heaped up, each needing twenty signatures and twenty different bribes before they were allowed through the customs. He could hear it all, they were sounds he would never forget, always carried inside his head. He felt jubilant at the thought that his revenge was being planned in that faraway and uncontrollable hellhole, where everything finished up, riches and rubbish, millionaires and the pirates in their pay. And there, in a rusting metal cube buried deep in the terminal of No. 2 Quay, Apapa in Badagry Creek, in the midst of thousands of other abandoned containers, in the boiling heat of filthy, pillaged, rubbish-strewn Africa, there, at the fingertips of a friendly little street urchin, was the detonator that would blow everything sky-high. It was a good feeling.

Another message appeared on the screen:

From: k35HYT@gmail.com
To: londonsubwaystreet@gmail.com
Subject: Re: Re: Egbe bere

@uche
K.

Kay had just given the detonator a Twitter name – it would be called Uche.

Once he was back in the street, Nwankwo couldn't help watching all the people around him. They were getting on with their lives, walking, bicycling, running, kissing each other, exercising the dog, arguing over trifles. He wanted to tell them all that a small guided missile was about to make the headlines, and that it would be arriving from Africa, that miserable continent where the inhabitants, long long ago, had believed that the first white men they saw were spirits, to be feared and respected. Nwankwo, so well brought up and respectable, was nonetheless almost drunk with anger. He was alone now with only Uche for company, and there was nothing more for him to do; but, like the worm in the middle of the fruit, he was close to his target.

He felt calmer the next day, sitting by the window on the TGV. He was leaving Paris after his three solitary days there. He closed his eyes, thinking about his son, who had fulfilled his mission, about his little girls and Ezima who were about to go and join him, about Lira and the strange night he had spent with her, about her extraordinarily direct way of speaking – he could never have talked like that, women just had this gift for seizing life as it came. He thought about his mother, travelling by train with her to visit the family when he was little. It had been a huge event, like going into space, for a child who had only known stony paths until then. That train had wound through a threatening landscape, peopled in his child's imagination, and perhaps in reality too, by ferocious wild beasts and moving spirits; at every station along the way his heart had beaten louder, echoed, it seemed, by the puffing of the train.

Eventually Nwankwo opened his eyes to see the French plains sailing past; the train ran like a well-oiled conveyor belt. Forests here were no more than thickets, and the only reminder of darker forces were the few grey church towers inhabited by an exhausted deity. There were too many comforting certainties in this landscape. *Don't you agree, Uche?*

THE SUN TSAR AT VERSAILLES

Le Canard enchaîné, 5th October

The Hall of Mirrors at Versailles has been closed to the public! In three days time, Sergei Louchsky will be holding his fortieth birthday party there. "Dom Pérignon champagne, caviar, 110 waiters for 48 tables, 14 chefs, 500 'medallion' chairs specially made for the occasion, 8,000 roses for the2 table settings and, for the floral decorations, 16,000 lilies of the valley with 7,600 water vases to hold them" – no expense has been spared. And one might add that the 500 guests are not just anyone, starting with the President himself, who declared on television a few days ago: "I will not let the State go bankrupt. This cannot go on. We must seek out growth wherever we can find it, in the Northern Caucasus if necessary." The Caucasus is coming to him this week, but he'll soon be rambling northwards.

When Steffy started telling him about how a lesbian friend of his, Pascale, had been inseminated with his sperm, and about what the custody arrangements would be if it succeeded, and how he was expecting the results of the pregnancy test at any moment, which was why he kept looking at his mobile, Félix finally exploded:

"So now you're just the same as everyone else!"

He said it as though Steffy had just announced that he had become heterosexual. Félix had always considered that announcing to his parents that he would never have a wife or children had been a decisive and revolutionary act. To him little arrangements with modern science that enabled gay people to push a pram were like a broken promise, a betrayal of all he stood for. That didn't prevent Steffy from carrying on in this febrile manner, grabbing his mobile every few minutes, turning it on, looking at it, putting it back in his pocket.

"Why don't you just leave it on the table, and then we can change the subject!" Félix suggested. He hadn't come to talk about nappies three days before Louchsky's coronation at Versailles.

"OK, so tell me about your trip to London…"

Félix did so, lying with a certain amount of inventiveness, describing shopping trips, parties, outrageous behaviour, Mark's friends, arguments they had had, the dilemma about their future together. Steffy listened, expertly winding his Thai noodles around his chopsticks.

"You're taking the piss," he suddenly said, looking up into Félix's eyes.

Félix stopped talking.

"The British secret services forwarded their reports to the DGSE. They're in a great state over there, about Louchsky.

I've got a mate there who recognized your name. From what he told me, I can't believe you had the time to go to all those exhibitions…"

"I see. So now I'm being spied on by my own friends."

"You should be thanking me! And, I might warn you, you're being watched here as well."

"What the fuck's going on in this stinking country?" Félix was getting angry.

"It's what I told you would happen! You started treading on forbidden ground. Over here they think Louchsky is Father Christmas. He's handing out money and jobs, so it's the red carpet, Versailles, anything he wants. So I would just move on, there's nothing to see here."

"Yes, of course, Versailles…"

"It's in three days' time. He'll have the Legion of Honour; there's a big dinner, fireworks, five hundred guests, the head of state, all the captains of industry, celebrities, they'll all be there. The tanks are rolling so get out of the way!"

"Go on, tell me who's coming – give me a laugh!"

"There are five hundred guests, I don't know them by heart."

"The entire government I suppose…"

"Almost. And Douchet's wife's in charge of the table plans, I think she runs an events-organizing company."

A light went on in Félix's brain. He tried to conceal it from Steffy. Douchet's wife. Hilar. The transfers. No, surely the sums were too large even for a party at Versailles. The events company must be a cover for the payment of some kind of commission.

"And they've got to leave room for the financial bosses," Steffy continued. "And for the British Prime Minister and his entourage, the African oil moguls, the actresses, the journalists. There are a lot of ruffled feathers among those who haven't been asked. My minister gets the most pathetic text messages."

"What about you, are you going?"

"I wrote the Minister's speech, but all I get is a pass to come into the grounds to watch the fireworks after the dinner. And don't expect me to smuggle you in, I don't want to crouch in the bushes watching the party."

"Just as well. If I plant a bomb at least I won't have your death on my conscience."

"Stop it, I'm going to start fancying you again – you'd make a very sexy Robin Hood!"

They both gave a forced laugh. In the past their lunches together had been funny and tender. They had exchanged little stories about the government, there had been vague yearnings and gestures which betrayed memories of their past relationship. Now each probably thought the other had changed. Steffy turned his mobile on again.

"I'm being careful," he said. "A lot of people know about you and me. They may have tapped my phone. Did you hear about what happened to your judge?"

"No!" Félix jumped.

He had left London too soon to receive the judge's letter. Steffy told him all the latest news from the Chancellery. Félix listened, frozen. He could hardly touch his food or look at his friend.

"You see, Steffy," he said finally, after a few moments, "I could never have predicted that it would be easier for me to be a gay man than a judge's clerk."

"Well, and I could never have predicted that I might become a father. We'll probably both end up as disenchanted as any heterosexual man. That's what you can't bear, Félix, you thought you were above all that."

A bit later, he added:

"Don't destroy your life. Look at your friend, that Russian journalist. At best she might be given the Sakharov Prize, at worst she'll get herself killed. And for what?"

Félix raised his eyes and stared at Steffy with utter contempt. He had just spoken about Lira like a civil servant in charge of giving a veneer to human rights at the Ministry.

He would be equally capable of producing an obituary or words of praise, it was all the same to him. It was just a matter of which pigeonhole to choose.

"And so, why isn't it her getting the Legion of Honour? Wasn't it once a medal given to members of the Resistance?"

"Look, I've no idea what it is you and your friends have got possession of that's putting those secret-service Brits into such a state, but I can assure you you haven't got the manpower," Steffy reiterated.

Silence fell between them. Then the news came: the insemination had been successful. Steffy was thrilled, but Félix was unable to share his joy. Soon they went their separate ways. Steffy asked Félix if he planned to go back to work. Félix lied – "Yes" – not sure if he would be believed.

He felt very distant now from this man whom he had loved in the past, and who was still trying to protect him. He had now drawn another line between himself and other people. He walked for a while, coming close to the area and then the street where his parents lived. He thought of paying them a surprise visit, but he remembered their last conversations on the telephone, and the way he always failed to say what they wanted to hear. So he continued on his way.

Round white tables were set like water lilies on a rippling pond; a low contented murmur rose up and echoed against the painted ceiling, eighty yards of military victories, and the political, economic and artistic triumphs of the long-gone France of the Sun King. And then there were the mirrors, which gave this gallery its name, three hundred and fifty-seven of them facing the windows, that evening reflecting long dresses, dinner jackets, rivers of diamonds, gleaming white teeth – all thought they could see in their reflection the fleeting image of a member of a ruling family.

Enter Sergei Louchsky. Forty years old today, with a falsely ecstatic grin on his face, his square head sitting hard and cold on his well-maintained body. His wife held his hand: she was ten years younger, with fine pale skin enhanced by the plunging neckline of a spangled midnight-blue ball gown. "Dior," a jealous murmur went up among the other wives. Not many young people there that night.

How they were envied, for their youth, their riches and the glamour they brought with them from a Moscow that had hitherto only exported ancient carcasses in Soviet uniform or bearded dissidents. Everybody stood aside to let them pass, a double hedge of people such as used to form at the passage of great noblemen. There had once been a masked ball held here after the wedding of Marie-Antoinette to the Dauphin; they had been mere children – their combined age was less than thirty – terrified at the thought of ending the evening alone together, naked under their nightshirts, behind the curtains of their four-poster bed. They didn't yet know that their heads would be cut off. Kings nowadays were more relaxed, the Revolution was well behind them, and now the Republic was paying

243

court to them, drawing up contracts – all they had to do was enjoy their power. And on top of all that Elton John was going to sing that night.

Louchsky advanced, greeting his guests. He tried to show warmth, even though everything in him breathed only power, business and predatory attack. His table was at the centre of the room. The palace historians had suggested placing it at the end of the gallery, by the Salon de la Paix; that was where the king's throne was installed on great state occasions, but the organizers had decided that the centre would appear more convivial, more modern. Tonight was the celebration of a new world, which borrowed nothing from the old one except its splendour. Louchsky continued his advance, clapping the shoulders of an important Champs-Élysées jeweller, a big American industrialist, the Minister of Defence Douchet (Mrs Louchsky snapped at him: "So where's the President?") and the Chelsea centre forward; he kissed the hand of an actress still glowing from her Oscar, and attempted a hearty joke with the number two in French luxury goods. He knew what good photos would come out of all this, little vignettes tossed to the press like crumbs or remains, for humble folk to pore over in the Métro.

But he was always looking elsewhere, busily scanning the crowd, that other mirror of power. They were all there, too, his future oil revenues, in the shape of the vice-president of the Brazilian oil company; as were the fund managers, the clever bloodhounds of the emerging economies, those "financial Mozarts" as *Paris Match* had described them, the twenty top names from the *Financial Times*'s most recent list of the hundred most powerful financiers in the world.

Governor Finley's smile was as wide as a chunk of trans-Saharan pipeline. He wasn't hard to spot, he was one of only ten black faces at the party, if one was only counting the guests. Of course the proportion was greater among the staff. That evening they had recruited waiters with big shoulders who were supposed to look like bodyguards and effortlessly whirled trays of champagne above the heads of the guests.

Finally Louchsky reached his table and sat down, a signal for everybody else to find their places. You could tell a lot from your position in this particular solar system. Vandel – the ex-president of the European bank who, since he retired, had been hired to advise the oligarch – had been punished by being placed close to the door, to his wife's fury: he should have anticipated the collapse of Grind Bank. French ex-golden boy Dellant realized then that he would now never get control of the Lagos container terminal, despite the fact that he ran forty other African ports. If he had been placed below Finley, it was because Louchsky wanted it that way. All he could do now was put up with his neighbour, a princess with a long nose, who was warmly congratulating him on his foundation against illiteracy. She seemed to know a lot more about it than he did.

Further away two art dealers who were famous enemies found themselves at the same table. "We've quarrelled, haven't we?" said one of them. The other answered: "Well, we've got one friend in common, I suppose." Anne Vuipert, the French President's special adviser and linchpin of the special relationship with Louchsky, would have preferred it if the photographer had not immortalized her proximity to the head of Goldman Sachs, whose compensation had just been made public: twenty-two million dollars for a year's work. She stiffened. At least she wouldn't be smiling in the picture.

Finally the President and his wife arrived, crossing the room with all the confidence of people delayed by important affairs of state. They sat down at Louchsky's table, alongside the British Prime Minister; Germany had sent its finance minister. The President wasn't going to speak at this birthday party that looked like a summit conference. He had done that earlier in the day in the Élysée drawing room when he made Louchsky a Commander of the Legion of Honour, and had declared "for the attention of cynics" that "just because you're friends doesn't mean your relationship is in any way unethical". Louchsky had much appreciated this blank cheque. He carried on insistently patting the President's shoulder, while the two official photographers bombarded them with their flashes.

It was the Foreign Minister who made the speech. For this occasion he chose to recall Peter the Great's visit to this palace. He launched off, his voice imitating the vibrating tones of television documentaries about royalty: "On the morning of the twenty-fifth of May 1717, the Tsar sailed on the Grand Canal. He visited the Menagerie and then the Trianon. He observed everything and noted all the things he wanted to reproduce in St Petersburg. One of the features he was most struck by, apart from the splendour of the palace, was the layout of the town itself. He reproduced the chessboard design with the three avenues radiating outwards. He also noted the width of the streets, at that time lacking in Paris itself…"

The boss of France's largest civil engineering company sat at his table devouring the bread rolls on his side plate just as he had devoured the public markets in St Petersburg. He smiled to himself – his cement was flowing over there, as though perpetuating the greatness of France. Beside him, Metton, a top consultant on the Parisian stock market, wondered how to tell him that he had poppy seeds stuck in his teeth. The Foreign Minister was now recalling the historic friendship between the French and Russian people, who had so often found themselves thrown together by the vagaries of history. It was the old diplomat's trick – putting "the people" in places where they had never been invited: "Was it not here, in this very gallery, that the Treaty of Versailles was signed, putting an end to the First World War?" The Minister was getting carried away; his face was turning scarlet.

"The Russians were Bolsheviks in those days, not quite the same thing as this!" snarled an old Goncourt-prize winner. His remark was met with severe looks from his table companions, who would not tolerate bad manners.

When the speech ended there was polite applause and the hors d'oeuvres began to arrive. It was eight-thirty.

"Osetra caviar, poached langoustines! Truffled egg mousse!"

Everybody began to concentrate on their plates and their neighbours. The wine waiters began their ballet. The women very soon became bored. Their shoulders, some better concealed than others, were glued to the backs of the chairs in order to allow the men on either side to talk across to one another. They sat there with vacant smiles and lost stares. They had trained themselves for this, having bought happiness through their husbands' business dealings; but they still cast envious eyes at the voluptuous Oscar-winning actress sitting right at the centre of the Louchsky solar system. She had declared just the other day in *Elle*: "I don't belong to the union of women who grow old." They would have loved to be able to say the same.

It was the self-made men who gave the loudest roars of laughter. They let themselves go more easily than those who had merely inherited their fortunes. Their conversation generally followed an autobiographical theme, summing themselves up: "My headmaster always told me: you'll end up either in prison or a millionaire. And I've done both!" said an American soft-drinks tycoon. And his French neighbour, who had made his fortune through hotlines and mobile phones, confessed through a mouthful of caviar that he had almost simultaneously received a Businessman of the Year award and a summons for fraudulent receipt of social benefits. They laughed comfortably together, savouring their success and crafty know-how.

"You know, we're only intermediaries," interrupted a banker at the same table. "He's the real thing." Pointing at Louchsky.

Every now and then the sound of a mobile would insinuate itself into the conversation. Nobody paid much attention, everybody had their own, in their jacket pocket or the evening bag that matched their dresses. It would ring, they would get it out, look at it, put it away. Sometimes they would look at the screen without it ringing, to read the latest messages, or to see how the stock markets were doing, the latest headlines, the Bloomberg alerts, the Twitter account. They were like pocket mirrors, one more reflection in this Hall of Mirrors. And so when the unknown Tweet arrived simultaneously on a dozen mobiles, nobody was particularly worried.

Rassmussen was the first to understand that something was happening. His eyes widened as he looked down at his screen, and he turned towards Louchsky, whose antennae immediately picked up the danger signal. Gradually, from table to table, conversations turned to whispers; people eyed one another nervously, seeking confirmation. Phones were now ringing everywhere, and everywhere the same message appeared:

RT@uche French defence minister taking bribes
http://lgoo.gt/UK71 #scandal

"Yeehaw!"

Kay gave a little shout. He had fired. He had sent out the first missile at 20.45, as instructed by Nwankwo. They were in the same time zone, so there could be no mistake. It had just taken one click and his Scud had flown off at the speed of light. He had been preparing the attack for several days with his counterparts in Abidjan and Nairobi. They had never met but he had already spent more hours in their company than he had with his own mother. This was the underground world of the African Internet. They weren't like the hackers and the little hooded geniuses of the West, they were just resourceful boys, capable of setting up an almost infinite number of mirror sites with programming so complicated that the Seattle technicians would be tearing their hair out. Kay drank the last of his can of Coke, and turned on his Afrobeat music. The next shot would be in fifteen minutes' time.

The organizers were scraping back their chairs. Some of them started by pushing out the two photographers, despite the fact that they had been hired to stay until the fireworks began. "What about the cake?" one of them said. "Out. Now!" Others rushed over to the representatives of the press who were signalling to one another: "Have you seen this?" And how – they'd seen it all right. One part of their brain was dialling the editorial offices to get the story in quickly, the other was working out how to leave without being noticed. Their legs were jiggling beneath the tablecloths in desperation to get going. All were staring over at the presidential table.

Their conversation had stalled. Rassmussen was whispering in Louchsky's ear. And the same was happening with the French President, who appeared to be tearing a strip off his adviser. The wife of the German minister appeared to be asking for more wine; her husband signalled to her that this wasn't the moment. Douchet got up, went over to the Prime Minister, shook his head, and then sat down again. His wife summoned the string quartet, earlier than planned, and told the wine waiters not to leave a single glass empty. People slowly began to relax again. It would be a shame, after all, not to finish the caviar – it was probably just some huge practical joke, a gang of extremists maybe, out to spoil the party. There were so many of them around these days.

21.06: new message on Twitter.

RT@uche video interrogation governor
http://bit.ly/le-V74as #british gov #compromised

From table to table you could see backs hunched over: the guests had their phones concealed in the folds of their dresses or under the tablecloth. They were downloading the link. It was a video, quite long. Soon nobody was speaking any more; everybody was watching the case full of banknotes being forced open, the governor issuing threats, Helen saying: *"Mr Finley, according to our sources, a governor in Nigeria earns twenty-five thousand dollars a year. You have just bought a house in Hampstead for fifteen million pounds. Can you explain this?"* And then the telephone ringing in the office, Helen turning pale, Finley triumphant.

Louchsky too was watching.

Finley rose from his seat. He alone knew what the word "uche" meant. He looked with fury at the back of the British Prime Minister, who was taking care not to move a muscle. The tall, proud figure stormed out of the hall. They all watched him go by, recognizing that snarling jawline from the video still running on their phones. Dellant fell in behind him, thinking this might be just the moment to corner the rights to the port of Lagos. Others watched. The feeling that they were at the right place at the right time had changed into an urge to get out as quickly as possible. Phones began to ring, the organizers ran to and fro, editorial offices were hotting up and soon the cameras and microphones would be at the gates of the palace of Versailles, demanding explanations.

Rassmussen charged into the kitchen, one hand holding his telephone, ringing anyone he could think of, as though the Internet were a tap that could be turned off, and the other waving at the staff, ordering them to serve the main course immediately. He brutally pushed the maître d' into the hall, where he announced: "Boned pigeon, stuffed with foie gras, with an olive *jus!*"

Outside, the first television and radio vans were drawing up and unloading their equipment. A call to march on Versailles had been launched on Facebook by a group of net-surfers called "Death to Corruption". The idea had caught on like wildfire. Those bankers, industrialists and politicians would have a party all right, cornered in the Hall of Mirrors, while the scandal spread throughout the whole information network, supported by videos and mountains of documents. Kay had done his job well.

Vandel, suddenly delighted at having been placed so near the door, got up quickly and left. The Brazilian oil tycoon did the same – after all, drilling hadn't yet begun in the bay of Santos. Several women followed, on the pretext of powdering their noses, tiptoeing in their stiletto heels, with their husbands behind them. Then the German Finance Minister got up. He left the top table, saying that he had an urgent call from the Chancellor. Louchsky nodded, but did not look up or shake his hand; he was watching the French President frantically signalling to his prime minister who was at the next table. The former seemed to be reminding the latter of an ancient constitutional custom: you're the connection, so you stay.

Night had fallen, cold, starlit and slightly threatening, as it so often does in the mountains. On the big oak table wine, bread and local sausage. Eight plates and eight glasses. Dmitry counted them in silence. He hadn't opened his mouth once that day, since the morning, when Nwankwo had arrived on the bus. He knew, she had warned him. He had shouted at her: "You've got no respect for anything! Not your daughter, not your friends, not me! You're the only one that counts, aren't you?" And then Félix had turned up that afternoon, accompanied by the judge. They made a strange pair, those two, complete opposites but inextricably bound together. Dmitry had remained silent throughout, deaf to Jacques's assurances that he, Jacques, was delighted to have some company in his house, and to Lira's protestations that she had no choice in the matter, that it was a question of life or death. He remained angry. She had turned this refuge that he had found for his daughter into a revolutionary cell.

He found it quite unbearable – their joy at seeing each other again, exchanging news, supporting Lira. He was irritated by Nwankwo's serious manner and Jacques's wife's exaggerated hospitality, all the trouble she was taking with these piles of plates and cutlery. As though they were just going to have a convivial dinner together. When the moment came for them all to sit down and raise their glasses at Jacques's signal, Dmitry banged down on the table with his fist.

"So we're drinking Lira's health, are we?"

"Shut up, Dad!"

"You're going to have to make a few wishes my girl! Your mother loves trouble and we don't count any more!"

"Shut up!"

"I've already told you, they've taken every precaution before coming here," Lira said calmly.

"What precautions? Look at yourself! Just look at yourself!"

"I can't—"

"That's what I'm telling you. What's the point of precautions? It's too late."

"Stop this, Dad!" Polina shouted, clutching her mother.

"If anyone loves you here, it's me," he said, his jaw trembling.

Nwankwo got up. He was holding his mobile, useless here, but he wouldn't let go of it.

"Dmitry," he said, "We're not madmen or heroes. We'll leave soon, I promise you. But we couldn't do anything else."

"And you don't think she's paid enough! She's blind, she can't annoy anyone any more, they'll leave her alone! But oh no, you're still there, glued to her, with your stench of death. So is that your thing then, tucking up blind people at night? This woman was my wife and she's the mother of my daughter – I'm responsible for her, so you can just bugger off!"

"I'm not your wife any more," Lira said.

She knew how hard it was for him to hear her saying it. Even in the dark, even mutilated as she was, she didn't want to be his wife. She would have liked to have been able to get up and replay one of the scenes that had preceded their separation and then go out slamming the door behind her. But she could no longer do that. From now on she would have to rely on sharp words, and leave the shouts and the crashing around and the slamming doors to others. Dmitry grabbed his jacket and his keys and left the room. A cold draught blew in and they all listened as the car drove off.

"He'll be back," Jacques said.

There was another beep, the alerts were flooding in now. Nobody bothered to turn off the ringtone any more. The Hall of Mirrors had turned into a gigantic call centre.

"Now what!" the French President cursed.

He got up, not waiting any more, and told Louchsky, who sat frozen on his chair, that he should do the same if he knew what was good for him. He left, followed by his wife. The British Prime Minister fell in behind him. They were falling like ninepins now. The smartphones were spewing out details of offshore accounts, conflicts of interest, bribes and commissions.

RT@uche Louchsky implicated in Grind Bank
http://bit.ly/lfUMLEg #corruption #bankruptcy

The ancient mirrors now reflected a half-empty room, the tables with their floral decorations now deserted, others with only two or three guests left. These too gradually rose and drifted away. The pigeon lay congealing on the plates. The marble pillars with their gilded capitals no longer seemed to be supporting anything. Louchsky, who just moments ago had been compared to the greatest of tsars, was now just the man of the present, an all too immediate present, which had become as flimsy as a cigarette paper. His wife tried to lay a comforting hand on his arm; he brushed it aside; his eyes seemed to have sunk in their sockets, a vein on his temple throbbed, he appeared to be silently screaming.

They were all jostling each other on the monumental staircases and in the cloakrooms, where everybody was shouting for his or her fur coat, hat or scarf. They all knew what awaited them outside. The most powerful guests had been allowed to bring their cars and chauffeurs into the courtyard, but the others were going to have to walk through the gates to find their limousines outside. "They're all lefties out there," they were muttering, "and journalists."

"Same thing!" shouted one angry woman.

And then it started to rain, first a fine mist, then a solid downpour. The luckier ones were able to hide behind the frosted windows of their cars; all they had to suffer were a few knocks to the bodywork, or microphones tapping on the glass. The others just had to join the departing procession on foot. There were miserable faces, crumpled suits, evening dresses weighed down by soaking hems; bankers searching for their chauffeurs, rich foreigners who didn't care about the French television cameras, law-and-order chiefs snarling with fury, and PR people still affecting a rictus grin when faced with outstretched microphones and machine-gunning flash photographers.

The police had called in reinforcements and were trying to form a protective cordon. The demonstrators pushed against it. "We want bread, we want bread," they chanted jeeringly. They had been yelling all the way from the RER station on the Avenue de Paris. Mobiles were working flat out, summoning more and more mates to the demo. The first images had already begun to appear on the Internet, short amateur films showing the mob, the militant chants and the police at bay.

It was now ten o'clock. One journalist, standing soaked to the skin in front of the gates, was speaking live on the radio:

"Where are all the stars, the politicians, the big bosses that we read about on the guest list? We don't see them coming out. The President's car, and the Prime Minister's are still parked in the courtyard. What is going on inside? We know nothing for the moment."

As if in reply, one of the demonstrators shouted: "There's another entrance! They're going to escape through the gardens!"

Then there was another beep.

RT@uche Grind Bank number two tortured to death.
http://bit.he/bgJMLOh #murder

Eyvin, all his secrets, his body lying in an English wood – the story was now spreading throughout the Twitter community. Blood was flowing now. Down below, the mob bellowed louder still. Up in the galleries, Madame Douchet sobbed into her napkin. The ambassador awaited his orders. The fine cheeses were wheeled in on chrome-plated trollies pushed by robotic head waiters.

Young Mrs Louchsky was urging her husband to leave, and so was the director of the palace. He offered them the escape route already taken by the President and the British Prime Minister. It was a hidden passage, far from the noisy, angry crowds whose roar could be heard beyond the windows of the Hall of Mirrors. Louchsky didn't reply. He rose, tipping back his chair and shouted:

"Who the hell is this fucking Uche? Find him!"

Kay peeped out of the top of the container. Nobody in sight. He heaved himself up onto the top, and leapt over to another and then another, moving expertly among these cubes which had been his home since he was two. When he had climbed high enough, he sat down and lit a cigarette. He felt good. He looked out over the lagoon, at the houses on stilts. That was where he had been born, although there was no official record of his existence. Back there, not so long ago, he used to pretend that a bottle and a broom handle were a guitar and a microphone. The night was full of sounds, people talking, women shouting, the hum of engines, sometimes gunfire – all the usual background noise.

He lay down, stretching out, with the sense of having accomplished his mission. He still looked like a child, he was only nineteen. He gazed up, wondering if the crane might crash down on top of him. It always seemed to be leaning dangerously. He remembered that there had been more stars when he was little; it wasn't that they had disappeared, it was just that Lagos had grown so much bigger – the business district had been extended onto an artificial island and now lit up the sky.

He would move to a new container the next day. It would be safer.

"I'd like to turn on the radio," Nwankwo said suddenly. He was like a nervous general awaiting news from the front.

Jacques obeyed without asking questions. First they heard the sound of a popular song, a glittering trifle totally unsuited to the occasion, almost disturbing in its frivolity. Jacques tuned through the airwaves searching for news, until he eventually found a crackling channel on which you could hear the sounds of demonstrators' shouts, people jostling one another, hooting and barracking, songs and revolutionary slogans.

"What's going on?" Lira cried.

"Listen!" Nwankwo said, not understanding what was being said any more than she did. He looked questioningly at Félix, who nodded and raised a triumphant thumb. A journalist was speaking live from the middle of the crowd. He was outside the Palace of Versailles, said he was awaiting the hurried departure of the President of France. He ended his report after a minute.

"Bingo! They're in the shit!" said Félix.

"What's happening?" Lira insisted.

"Well, Lira," Nwankwo began, rather solemnly, "I didn't tell you anything because nothing was certain, and I didn't want you to be disappointed again. There's a kid I know in Lagos who's put everything we know on Twitter. He's sending out a scoop every fifteen minutes. So it's all going belly-up at the dinner in Versailles. They all know now – all the media people, all the politicians all over the world – they all know what sort of a man Louchsky is."

"You mean—"

"I mean they know about the French Minister's kickbacks! They know he has blood on his hands! They know about Grind Bank's money-laundering activities!"

Sometimes these things leave you speechless – huge pieces of news, a final revenge or a too-long-awaited miracle. Lira sat frozen on her chair, letting Nwankwo's words wash over her, trying to imagine this magic thread that was sending their secrets from Africa to the Versailles dinner tables. Nwankwo went over to her and placed his hand on her shoulder, a simple but deeply tender gesture – was it the night they had spent together that allowed it, or just this hard-won victory? Perhaps both. "He'll pay dearly for what he did to you, the world will know him for what he is," he murmured.

At the other end of the table, Félix was explaining to the judge and to Jacques and his wife what was happening. But he watched Lira from the corner of his eye, imagining the thoughts going through her head. He wanted to laugh, and above all he wanted to see her laugh.

"When I think that Finley must be plunging his fish knife into the British Prime Minister's back!"

"So you knew?" Lira said.

"A little. But not everything. I tell you, Nwankwo's a solo player. Brilliant work Nwankwo!"

And he raised his glass, erasing all traces of their earlier quarrel in London. He cursed out loud at this house with its lack of Internet and its wind turbine. They could have watched their victory spreading like wildfire. Jacques just laughed. His wife offered him some more roast lamb.

"Just do what I do, use your imagination!" Lira retorted. She was a little drunk now.

Polina kept looking towards the door in the hope that her father might reappear. She smiled at her mother's happiness, kissed her and let herself be kissed, but she always remained a little apart, on the edge of the story. The judge, too, was simply observing the scene, but from another angle, that of the older generation. He was like an artisan watching his particular skill becoming redundant. That evening he had no regrets about leaving the law courts – justice was taking a different route now. Jacques and his wife saw to it that plates were laden and glasses filled; their eyes shone with pride at the fact that they were sheltering this scarred, united and fearless group, but they felt a cloud of anxiety, too, as they saw how vulnerable the lives of those assembled around their table were. Nwankwo, Lira and Félix formed a unified block in the eyes of the others, linked together by all those days they had spent together poring over figures, the fear, the doubts they had had about one another – it had all added up to a secret and unique experience that only they could understand.

Two famous newspaper columnists wandered around together in the Bosquet de l'Obélisque, bemoaning the fact that the pace of the news meant that one could no longer dine and write leaders in peace and at one's own pace. A man ran up behind them. It was the Prime Minister's press attaché; the Prime Minister wanted to see them straight away. One of the wives stood shivering over by the Bosquet du Rond-Vert, begging her financial-wonder-boy husband to get their little private jet to land on the Versailles lawn. By the fountain of Apollo a socialist deputy yelled at his chauffeur – if he wanted to keep his job he would do well to master the satnav and find a way out pronto. He lowered his voice when he saw other lost guests heading towards the fountain. He recognized one of them, the consultant Metton, an old friend from university and student activist days. He went over to him.

"How can we get out without being seen?"

"There's only one way – the Trianon, Petit or Grand, they're in the same direction. It's where the kings and queens used to fuck their lovers, there must be a way out towards Paris…"

The deputy didn't ask himself whether the layout might have changed somewhat after three centuries, he just followed his friend out of habit. They took a right-hand fork, and ran into the firework engineers who stopped them and told them to turn back; there were rockets and explosives all over the place, they were in a danger zone.

"I think you'll find the firework display will be cancelled," the deputy said.

No. Louchsky was on the terrace. He now had only about thirty people around him. The Kremlin had called, ordering him to come home. He had replied that he would be back early the next morning. His plane was waiting at the Saint-Cyr aerodrome, just behind the park of the palace. If this was the moment of his downfall, it was the moment to leave his mark on the sky of Versailles. He ordered the firework display to be launched. The director wondered out loud whether this would be appropriate given the situation, but he backed away fast under Louchsky's scorching glare.

Soon sparkling bouquets rose and exploded above the park and the palace, yellow, purple, red, blue and green, first separate and then mingled. The sky above Versailles lit up, visible for miles around, with loud explosions that seemed designed to drown out the sound of demonstrations and gathering rumours.

At the same time newspapers were junking their first editions and preparing new headlines. The printers were churning out banners about a government scandal; meanwhile the Élysée crisis unit was poring over the revelations and issuing frantic denials. The same thing was happening at the Quai d'Orsay, where Steffy watched as the Minister arrived back screaming with rage at these "little Internet fuckers". He thought of Félix. He knew perfectly well that he and his friends were behind all this. In London Helen was woken up by the non-stop ringing of her telephone. In Nice, the prosecutor left a dinner party in a hurry, asking for the judge's private number – he wanted to assure him of his great esteem.

As the final display exploded in a blaze of pyrotechnic skill, the Prime Minister, who was still ensconced in the king's apartment, was whispering to a small group of senior journalists that he had always warned the President about this over-successful Russian. Madame Douchet wandered through the Hall of Mirrors, stroking the bronze chandeliers. Outside, the diehard demonstrators yelled in unison with the rockets; the soaking journalists asked where the

President could have got to – his car was still in the court-yard – and the socialist deputy and his old university pal had taken refuge in the Temple de l'Amour, between the Petit Trianon and the Hameau de la Reine.

Louchsky's plane took off for Moscow.

Kay was now fast asleep in his container.

They left a huge pile of newspapers on the table, "For the fire," they said as they left. Jacques would quite like to have kept them, as they told the whole story of the hurricane they had lived through.

His invisible house was now empty, and he and his wife were alone together again. He looked out at his garden, at his wind turbine, at the slow and silent life that he had chosen for himself. He saw the bed of dying hollyhocks, the plump lettuces, the purple artichokes in front of the door, the light fading over the peaks and the footpaths winding above past the caves and tombs that had served as hiding places in so many wars over the centuries.

Jacques had built a lot of sets during his working career. He could produce a ship's hold, a minister's antechamber, a school dormitory, an eighteenth-century boudoir or a colonial brothel; he could plan it all, the moment when the door would slam, the wind rise, or a bomb would explode – that was what filming was all about. And yet he could not understand what had just been happening in his own house. He had seen Nwankwo marching down to the village with a telephone card at exactly four o'clock in the afternoon, and returning an hour later. And then that evening Versailles had exploded and the government had become engulfed in scandal.

The following morning they had all gathered around the radio, beaming and laughing. Dmitry had returned. Official denials were pouring in. Specialists were analysing the revelations; the opposition was calling for heads to roll; all the talk was of corruption; it looked as though Douchet would resign; Louchsky's shares had gone into free fall; the

Kremlin had removed him from control of the Russian state naval-construction company. And the United States had declared him *persona non grata*.

When Félix had translated one leader-writer's question: "But who or what is Uche? Some kind of secret organization?" Nwankwo had cried.

The judge had laughed hysterically when he found a small box in *Nice-Matin* referring to Linda Stephensen's death in Nice. "Was this story filed away too quickly?" the paper asked.

Jacques couldn't help thinking that as well as being dishonest they were pretty stupid to have left so many traces, but he kept that thought to himself. Because as the hours went by something seemed to be happening to his guests: the curious osmosis between them took the form first of a rush of ecstatic happiness, which grew fast and then seemed to wither away almost at once, as though crushed under mounting anxiety. Their new-found leisure allowed a hitherto forbidden question to be asked: what now?

One by one, they left. Lira, Polina and Dmitry had been the first to go, like a normal family, back up to Paris in their car. The university term was about to begin, Polina was enrolled again but under a different name. Then Félix had set off towards Nice with the judge. Nwankwo had gone alone, taking the bus to the station. Jacques had driven him to the bus stop. There were a lot of things he would like to have asked, starting with who Uche was, but he just shook his hand for a long moment, and told him that he would always be welcome.

As he climbed back up to his house, he had the feeling that he must now empty his mind. He thought he might go walking the next day, or the next, he would go past the Lac de Pise and climb up to the Col de l'Homme Mort: up there you felt so small and yet so high up, you wondered who the dead man was and why he died, and then you went down again without ever knowing. A neighbour shouted as he went by: "Hey you're getting a lot of visitors these days." He didn't reply, he just smiled and thought to himself that it might be a good idea to burn those papers after all.

My dear Lira,

We all miss you here at the magazine. We've been thinking of you, and of the darkness that surrounds you. How I wish I had never let you go.

The next edition will be out next week. You probably heard from Dmitry that soon after you were attacked our offices were ransacked and all the computers were stolen. The magazine has not appeared for two months. But now everything is back in place. Your office is intact and looks as though you are just about to walk in. But your desk is covered in letters, dozens arrive for you every day, from all over the world, from people you have met and from total strangers. They all express their admiration and sympathy for you. We will publish a selection in every future edition. There won't be a single one in which you are not mentioned. I must also tell you that your salary will go on being paid, 25,000 roubles per month. As long as I am in this chair, you are on my staff.

Dmitry tells me that you hate our country and that you will never set foot here again. I can understand that, but things might change. Everything can change.

Louchsky did not suffer any public humiliation, there was no pen thrown at him in front of the cameras, no pictures of him signing his resignation with a lowered head. Such images would have done nothing for those in power, bribery doesn't shock anyone here – nobody cares if the French government had been bought. We learnt from a communiqué that Louchsky was no longer at the head of the naval company.

He's still got a huge empire, he's very rich but no longer powerful. Here people laugh at him, that never happened before, everybody was too scared. And meanwhile there are incredible stories going round about the dinner at Versailles, some so extraordinary that they can't possibly be true. But it doesn't matter, it does people good. Something fundamental has changed in the way people regard him, both in and out of the Kremlin. Nothing you have done has been in vain, Lira. You ruined his coronation.

All the same I would do anything to turn the clock back, and to see you again marching into the office in a rage, like before, and this time I would say no, a hundred times no, to all your demands.

I was unable to protect you from the rage that devoured you then. I hope some of it is still there, making you as strong as ever, but this time, please, keep it for yourself alone.

I hug you, Lira. And so does everybody here.

Igor

When Nwankwo arrived back in London, the customs officer asked him to follow him into his office. A policeman came in and informed him that his residency permit had been rescinded, as had his post at the university, and that he was under arrest for theft on the premises of the Serious Fraud Office. Nwankwo listened calmly to all this, as though he was just letting himself be carried along, as though finding himself under arrest was the ultimate stage of the journey embarked upon by the ex-head of the Nigerian fraud squad.

Late that afternoon he appeared before a judge who would pronounce on whether he would be extradited, placed in detention or allowed out on bail. The judge asked him to be seated, and gently took his glasses out of their case, almost regretfully, as though extremely reluctant to pass sentence on a hero. He cleared his throat before each question. This man he was supposed to be judging had the looks of a stranger, but none of the fear that usually showed on the face of the hunted men he normally saw, who seemed like children in the dark; he had nothing in him of those miserable men who had thought they could find a better life in another country. There was something quite different about Nwankwo's expression – an incandescent stare that was hard to look back at, as though his exile was already complete and internalized.

Nwankwo replied to the questions. Yes, he admitted having copied the film before leaving the premises of the Serious Fraud Squad; yes, he knew Lira Kazan, but he had heard nothing from her since leaving her in Paris at the Gare du Nord with her husband. Félix? No that name meant nothing to him. The judge showed him the reports from the secret-service team in charge of the Oxford surveillance operation.

Nwankwo acted the fool. "Oh yes, that was a friend of Lira's. He came to see her. I had forgotten his name." Nwankwo felt no compunction in lying here, as so many had done before him. He was just waiting for one question, one single question. Finally it came. The judge said:

"Does the name Uche mean anything to you?"

And then Nwankwo beamed happily, like someone who knows but won't betray a comrade. Thanks to an @ sign Uche's wanderings were over. He could finally rejoin the world of the spirits who haunted the roads and paths by night.

In the end the judge granted him bail. Nwankwo returned to the Oxford house. Once again there was a policeman outside. Some of Lira's strings were still stretched along the walls. Nwankwo was now just waiting to be deported. He heard about Helen's resignation on the television. She held a press conference, refusing to testify against Nwankwo. She praised his expertise and knowledge of the law, and she gave the name and position of the person who had yelled at her over the telephone on the video which had now been seen by millions on the Internet. He was the Prime Minister's legal adviser, she said.

Nwankwo listened in amazement. He didn't hear Ezima coming in. She had knocked at the door, entered and was looking around this house that she had once thought was hers. He finally turned around, smiled sadly, and got up without approaching her. She had that closed expression that he knew so well; she refused the chair he offered her. She appeared to have rehearsed what she proceeded to say:

"I know Tadjou took something for you. You put your own son in danger. I don't want you coming anywhere near the children."

"Everything I have ever done has been for their sake," Nwankwo repeated. It was as though they were just repeating an old conversation.

"Stop it," Ezima sighed.

He approached. She backed away.

"So are you leaving then?" he asked.

"Yes, we're going home, we should never have followed you. I know I insisted on coming and I was wrong. I hadn't realized what you were capable of."

"Don't stay in Lagos, or in Abuja. Go across the border to your cousin. Finley will be like a madman."

"Tell the uncle where you are. He'll know where we are."

Then she left without waiting for an answer.

Speech by the President of the French Republic,
Saint-Nazaire, 22nd October

My fellow countrymen,

I have come here to see for myself that work has begun again. It is what I promised you, and therefore it has happened. This contract between our dockyards and the Russian naval-construction company marks the beginning of a new era. Two ships have been commissioned, and others will follow on the order book. I promise you that. The presence at my side of the Russian Vice-President is proof of Russia's long-term commitment to this project. I have always been scrupulous about one thing and that is to fulfil my promises to you. You can examine every commitment I have made. I have never lied to you.

I know that there were doubts and criticisms when I announced that I would not abandon you. And I have heard the rumours. There are documents in circulation, are they genuine or forgeries? It hardly matters, rumour has done its work. A young Russian captain of industry was unjustly blamed after the bankruptcy of an obscure bank. A minister of the Republic was forced to resign in order to defend his honour. There will be a judicial inquiry. It will discover nothing, because there is nothing to discover. In the past plotters would work in the back rooms of bars, now they spread rumours on the Internet. I say no to the rule of anonymous denunciation! Yes to the Republic! Yes to a France of the twenty-first century! What do these agitators know of the six months you have just spent on the dole? If the day comes when there are no dockyards, no factories, how will you live, how will your wives and your children live? You who are the first in line for delocalization? These cowards hiding behind their computers are betting on your death! I am placing my bet on your future, on your irreplaceable skills. I am placing my bet on the industrial future of our nation.

I have always believed in the future of shipbuilding, in your competence and I will never accept its disappearance. Here before you all today I wish to reiterate wholeheartedly the core values of our great nation, inscribed over all the monuments of this republic ever since our great revolution: Liberty, Equality, Fraternity.

I have only your interests at heart. Thank you.

"Madame, I am afraid that there is a profound necrosis and we will have to consider the removal of the eyes. After that you can decide whether to insert glass eyes, or leave the sockets empty and close the eyelids..." Lira fainted. The doctor's voice, and that of the interpreter, and Polina's involuntary cry of horror seemed far away. Lira imagined her eyes rolling out of her head, she saw the empty sockets, she saw herself dead and buried.

When she came round, she was lying in an empty examination room. Polina was talking to her in a gentle voice, stroking her forehead, and she heard a nurse's voice too, interrupting, saying that she needn't worry, that it was a normal reaction. Lira lay there in silence. Only Polina's words could reach her now.

"You had blue eyes, Mum. I need them to be blue again, even if they're glass ones. You should have the operation."

And so Lira agreed and the operation was fixed for two weeks later. Polina wrote down the date in her student diary. The days passed, each one the same, in their new apartment in a red-brick building south of Paris, near the campus of Polina's university. It was like a countdown to the operation.

Lira kept asking herself, sometimes quietly, sometimes out loud, why the loss of her eyes seemed so unbearable, when she had already lost her sight. It was a question that had no answer, for her, or for others. Tanya rang from St Petersburg; Lira could visualize her apartment, all that mess on the table, and both of them sitting on the floor not so long ago. Her parents rang too, begging her to come home. Never, she said.

Every day Polina came back with a new promise.

"You'll be able to write and look at the Internet, using a computer with a voice synthesizer. I went to a demonstration, it's brilliant. And you'll be able to run, there are people with dogs who will accompany you. You'll even be able to carry on with the karate, I've found a club for blind people—"

"Stop," Lira would say gently. She was haunted by the thought of the operation, and she couldn't bear any pity or compassion. She was drowning in nostalgia, and she had nightmares too. It was as though a part of her was about to be removed along with her eyes, as though they contained all her memories.

"When I was little they said I looked like a doll, because I was blonde and had blue eyes. Now I really will look like one with my glass ones. But I never liked dolls."

Félix came to see her on his way to London. He had left the law courts and was going to join Mark, hoping he would get through customs without any trouble. Lira fell into his arms and stayed there a long time, silent and fragile, something she had never wanted to be in the past. She asked him if he had any news of Nwankwo.

"He was deported eight days ago. I don't know where he is. But I'm quite sure he'll get in touch before too long."

"I'm frightened, Félix."

"I know."

"It's like putting my head on the block."

"No, Lira. You've been through the worst. I've never known anyone as strong as you."

"Do you really think we'll hear from Nwankwo?"

"I'm positive we will."

The operation went well. They cleaned out and emptied Lira's eye sockets, bandaged them and prepared for the implant of two deep-blue glass eyes.

When Lira, still unconscious, was wheeled out of the operating theatre, all that remained on the chrome table, waiting to be thrown away, were two small spheres, white,